Dancing with Lyndon

Also by Donley Watt

Can You Get There from Here?

The Journey of Hector Rabinal

Haley, Texas, 1959

Reynolds

a novel by

Donley Watt

TCU Press • Fort Worth, Texas

Library of Congress Cataloging-in-Publication Data

Watt, Donley.
Dancing with Lyndon : a novel / by Donley Watt.
p. cm.
ISBN 0-87565-280-8 (alk. paper)
1. Judges–Election–Fiction. 2. Johnson, Lyndon B. (Lyndon Baines), 1908-1973–Fiction. 3. Attorney and client–Fiction. 4. Trials (Rape)–Fiction. 5. Racism–Fiction. 6. Texas–Fiction. I. Title.
PS3573.A8585D36 2003
813'.54–dc21

2003007033

Cover Art/Lynn Watt
Book Design/Margie Adkins West

To the memory of my parents.

Chapter One

On a Saturday late in May of 1948 Thomas Patterson sat stiffly at the dining table in his house, sipping his cup of black coffee. He rapidly scanned the morning paper from front to back, then frowned and went through it once again, more slowly this time, from back to front. From the dining table he could hear his wife Mary Lee as she prepared breakfast a half-dozen steps away in the adjacent kitchen. But Thomas did not look up to watch her. As he did every morning of his life, he waited for Mary Lee to scramble his eggs and fry his bacon and butter his toast. He preferred his eggs soft-scrambled, his bacon crisp with no rubbery, fatty edges, and his toast lightly browned.

But while he waited, he could not help but hear Mary Lee struggling in the kitchen–the way she rushed frantically from stove to toaster, her slight but fervent incantations and protestations. Finally, Thomas smelled the unmistakable mingling of blackened toast and charred bacon, quickly followed by the scrape of knife on toast, and he could visualize the blackened crumbs as they scattered like burnt-out stars into the white porcelain sink.

Thomas sighed. You would think she could get it right after sixteen years. He lifted his eyes over the top of the paper, still avoiding the frantic scene in the kitchen, but hoping to find his own exasperation mirrored in the face of their son who sat across the table from him. But Tommy was lost in the comics, a bemused grin fixed on his face, Mary Lee's stewing and stirring and scraping no more an intrusion into his life than Blondie's fussing at Dagwood Bumstead.

Thomas withdrew even deeper into the paper, refusing to give in to his impatience, while he waited for his breakfast. He waited, also, for the black telephone in the hallway to ring. A phone call that would, he believed, change the direction of his life. Thomas Patterson's intuition as a lawyer hardly ever failed him, and it was right on target in this instance, but not at all in the way he expected.

While he waited, he hid behind the *Tyler Morning Telegraph*, concealing as best he could his pride. Even though Tyler was thirty-six miles to the east, the paper covered the events in the surrounding communities–including Cottonwood, where Thomas and Mary Lee and their son Tommy lived–and this day surely was significant enough for some small mention. Perhaps Thomas Patterson would find his name in an article. But so far he had come upon nothing.

It may have been early and a Saturday, but Thomas Patterson wore his best summer suit, the seersucker suit coat hanging from the curve of a hall tree in the entry of the house, along with an assortment of his summer straw hats. To protect his shirt and trousers, he had tucked into his collar a giant dishtowel that now draped his shirt and tie and lap.

The windows along the back of the house let in a light spring breeze that fluttered and then lifted the half-curtains that Mary Lee had sewn herself. Their next-door-neighbor Odie Mae Harwood was feeding a gathering of feral cats again in her backyard, and Thomas told himself to ignore the high-pitched yowling and Odie Mae's ceaseless calling. A chorus of yelps from farther down the street answered the cats, and Thomas steeled himself trying to keep his focus on the newspaper. This too shall pass, he thought. And it would, for the sun would soon send Odie Mae back indoors where she would seclude herself behind tightly drawn curtains, only to emerge with her cans of cat food early the next morning.

But a catfight broke out just then, and Odie Mae began banging on a tin dish, trying to break it up. "Can't you do something about that?" Thomas said, raising his voice so that Mary Lee, even in the kitchen, would have to hear him. "Do we have to put up with this every morning of our lives?"

Tommy turned from the comics and stared out the window. Mary Lee ignored her husband.

Oh, well, he thought, regaining his composure. It will be a lovely day, it appears, the morning temperate and then the afternoon hot. But what else could one expect in East Texas? At least there would be no rain to spoil what promised to be the most significant day of Thomas Patterson's life.

Across from Thomas, fourteen-year-old Tommy–who for his own reasons was impatient to start this day–lightly tapped a fork on the oak tabletop.

The fork was silver–not silver plate–with ornate leaves running down the handle, the silverware passed on to Mary Lee in a mahogany velvet-lined chest from her paternal grandmother, who had died some years back. The silverware fit into Mary Lee's grand plan, her strategy for the Pattersons to rise above the ordinary residents of Cottonwood, Texas. So silverware graced the table at every meal, even breakfast, and always cloth napkins, soft cotton napkins with crocheted trim, folded in curved triangles that stood up on the smooth table. And Honey Lee china, with a bouquet of pink, purple, and blue flowers in the center of each swirl-edged plate. That was Mary Lee's wedding china. The matching sugar bowl and salt and pepper shakers stayed on the table all the time. The sideboard held small china bowls for the condiments–the ketchup and mustard and mayonnaise. The bottom of a ketchup bottle had never touched the top of her table. A matter of principle, she maintained. In Mary Lee's mind these little touches added up.

Of course, the silver had to be polished, and the napkins had to be washed and then ironed, but that was Elberta's chore–Mary Lee drove north across the tracks every Thursday to pick the woman up. An extra household expense that she insisted was worth every penny, and Thomas had grudgingly agreed.

Some Thursdays, now that it was summer, Tommy drove his mother to get Elberta, the Ford rattling across the Cotton Belt railroad tracks, turning left at the "Quick-Toe Step Way" corner store. They followed the narrow dirt streets past the Negro high school, until they pulled to a stop and honked the horn for their maid.

Her house was a box of unpainted wood planks; a few old cans and pots–empty one gallon paint cans and broken-handled stew pots and a rusty bucket or two–held zinnias and marigolds and petunias on the front porch. A ramshackle outhouse leaned to one side out back, past the hand-dug well. Even in the summer Elberta brought into the car an intense aroma of wood smoke and fried pork. She was a large woman and grunted and sighed as she worked her way into the back seat of the two-door sedan. The car rocked on its springs when finally she settled in. As they drove off, the last wisps of smoke from her kitchen woodstove curled above a pipe that stuck out of the tin roof.

Elberta had cleaned on Thursdays as long as Tommy could remember, and he welcomed the calm that seemed to pervade their house when Elberta was around. For that one day a week, his mother seemed to set aside her impatience with his father.

While Tommy tapped the fork, he stared through the doorway and on into the living room where the big Philco radio dominated one wall. Tommy was lost, back reliving the night before when the three of them had spent most of the evening listening to "Fibber McGee and Molly" and "The Adventures of Sam Spade." When the "Green Hornet" came on, his father terminated the evening's entertainment with a click of the knob. "Ridiculous," he had muttered.

Tommy had asked his father when they could get a television set–there was one in the window of Farley's Furniture Store just off the downtown square. The snowy picture rolled and zigzagged, but Tommy could stand and watch for hours. "When they show 'Father Knows Best' on the television," Thomas had answered, "then I will consider it. But not before."

"Son." His father's stern voice suddenly jarred Tommy back to the breakfast table where he still idly tapped his fork. "Please. That tapping will drive me batty." He peered over the newspaper and over the half-glasses that hung on the end of his nose. He gave his head an almost indiscernible wag accompanied by a frown. Tommy stopped.

As he went back to his newspaper, Thomas announced, loudly enough for Mary Lee to hear, "Governor Jester will be here, you know. He will be speaking at one this afternoon. A fine way to start off the festivities, I would say." His voice was animated, because Beauford Jester, a native of nearby Corsicana, would show up to kick off Cottonwood's annual Old Fiddlers' Contest with a speech. Thomas, the up-and-coming candidate for state district judge and perhaps Shawnee County's next Democratic chairman–if old Robert Newsome, the county attorney, would ever call it quits–would introduce the governor.

Governor Jester's endorsement of Thomas' candidacy was probable, an endorsement that would all but assure the judgeship for Thomas in July's Democratic primary. There would be no opposition after that–oh, perhaps a sore-headed independent or a few write-in ballots–but in 1948 in Texas there would be no Republican opposition.

Thomas Patterson announced Governor Jester's visit as if it had not been known for weeks, announced it in a general sort of way, although the only ones to hear it in the modest white frame house on South Prairieville Street were his wife and son.

Tommy sighed impatiently. He already knew that the governor would be there and that his father would make some kind of appearance, and he figured that it would be boring. But he would go–he knew that he should go–so that he could tell his father later, without lying, that he had observed the ceremony and heard his introduction.

"And Lyndon Johnson," Thomas said, then cleared his throat of some morning congestion. Once more he raised his voice for Mary Lee's benefit. "Yes, Congressman Johnson, the Senate candidate, is scheduled to show up later in the day. A reception will be held this evening, out at the country club." When neither his wife nor son responded, Thomas peered over his newspaper once again. His combed-straight-back hair gleamed in the morning light. He smelled of Vitalis hair tonic mixed with a splash of Old Spice aftershave. "That Johnson should never have run against Coke Stevenson," he went on. "Why he did that, I will never know. He doesn't stand a ghost of a chance."

"Are you for Lyndon Johnson, anyway?" Tommy asked. "I mean officially?"

"Officially neutral. For now." Thomas folded the newspaper and set it aside. "I plan to discuss the congressman's candidacy with the governor, if I get the chance. I feel that Coke Stevenson might be the strongest candidate. He knows his way around. But sometimes it's best to wait and see."

Mary Lee hurried into the room just then, carrying a plate of burned and scraped toast and a percolator of coffee. She stopped and released an audible sigh, one that Thomas ignored. From the kitchen she had heard her husband's every word. "Coke Stevenson is fine," she said at last, sliding the plate of toast across to Tommy and finding a hot pad for the percolator. She felt herself becoming too busy, too hurried, unsure of what she wanted to say. "Yes, he is fine, if you want a horse-and-buggy senator."

Thomas slowly refilled his coffee cup and reached for a piece of toast. He noticed the charred edges and shook his head.

Back in the kitchen, Mary Lee furiously stirred a skillet of eggs, then moved back towards the dining room shaking an egg-coated spatula while she spoke. "Times are changing, Thomas. This is not 1930. It is 1948. The war is over, and we need to look to the future. We need young men to lead us."

She retreated to the stove but before long bounced back into the dining room with a platter of eggs and bacon. "We need young men. Like you, dear," she said, but didn't look at her husband.

Thomas glanced at his son, a boy that he hoped shared his own disposition, his careful and almost always accurate assessment of the facts. If only the boy could ward off the influence of his mother, he thought. He approved of Tommy, the way he always wore crisply starched shirts (thanks to Elberta), with his jeans' legs rolled two turns. And Thomas had not allowed his son to get a "burr cut," which all of the boys seemed to be getting, influenced by the return from the war of their GI fathers and uncles and older cousins.

Because of his age–when the Japanese bombed Pearl Harbor Thomas had already turned thirty–he had not been called up and he had escaped the troop mentality that so many of the veterans brought back home. No, Tommy wore his dark brown hair neatly trimmed, a precise part running down the left side. Tommy would develop into a gentleman, like his father.

Having grown up in Dallas put Thomas at an advantage in Cottonwood. He would see that Tommy didn't backslide into the ubiquitous country ways. He spread some plum jelly on a triangle of toast, carefully covering the edges. "Sometimes on these issues it is best to wait and see," he finally said, glancing up at his wife. "Until you have all the facts, all the information."

"Or wait and see which way the wind is blowing," Mary Lee said. She bent to spoon hard clumps of eggs onto three plates and passed them around. Her robe opened slightly, and Thomas caught a glimpse of her nightgown, the beginning of the curve of her breast. He quickly looked away.

"Oh, Thomas," she said, lightly touching his arm, the slightest gesture of affection possible. "Sometimes your caution drives me crazy!"

Then the phone rang, and Thomas carefully pulled the dishtowel from his collar. He folded it precisely and placed it beside his plate, next to the still-folded cloth napkin and, with obvious relief, he slid his chair back and stood.

"That," he said, "may well be the governor of Texas." Before he hurried to the living room, he gave Tommy a quick glance, hoping that his son would see from this exchange with his wife that reason always prevails.

Under the table Mary Lee made a fist, her nails cut into her palms. She rolled her eyes at Tommy, but the effects were wasted on her son, who refused to look up. He was taking forever to scrape the last drop of wild plum jelly from a serving bowl. Please don't let him grow up to be like his father, she prayed to no one in particular. And then she caught herself. It wasn't right to draw Tommy in; she didn't want–or need–for him to take sides. He would soon see–anyone would see–that Thomas behaved unreasonably in his reasonableness. No, that was not quite it. But she couldn't make sense of her feelings of anger at her husband.

Three weeks before, an aide to Governor Jester had called. Would Thomas introduce the governor when he came to

Cottonwood? “An honor,” Thomas had said. Then he hesitated. “Does this indicate the governor’s endorsement of my candidacy?” he asked. The phone had gone silent. Then Thomas heard a muffled exchange in the background.

Finally the aide came back on the line. “The governor’s visit is not of a political nature, therefore an endorsement at that time would be inappropriate. But at a future date an endorsement is a reasonable possibility.” Horsefeathers, Thomas had thought. He was no fool. He knew behind the scenes maneuvering when he saw it.

Well, I’ll show them, he thought now as he answered the phone.

Mary Lee hoped the call was not for her, not while Thomas was still at home. Just last week she had talked to Byron Bostick after church and casually mentioned her interest in the real estate business. Bostick Real Estate was the number one real estate enterprise in the county, and Byron had said he would call her in a week or so. “Maybe we can get together for coffee,” he said. His voice, as Mary Lee remembered it, came across as a little too conspiratorial, and his eyes moved up and down Mary Lee’s blouse a little too freely. She had had second thoughts and wondered if her boldness might have been misconstrued.

But it was not Byron Bostick on the phone. She could tell by the formal intensity of Thomas’ measured words.

Then from the living room Thomas’ voice rose. “No!” he said. “I don’t believe it!” His voice quivered despite his attempts to stay in control. “Oh, Lord help us.”

Now Tommy did meet his mother’s eyes, and they shared that moment, and he would remember it forever.

Later, when Tommy was older, he would confirm in photographs that Mary Lee Patterson was attractive then, in her late thirties. Slender and tall–as tall as her husband–with pronounced cheekbones that gave her face a layered, shadowed look. But her eyes set her apart. Not their color, an ordinary green-grey, but their spark, their promise of liveliness that reflected some inner condition that Tommy could not for a long time quite place. Optimism, he thought then, or hopefulness, maybe. And undoubtedly both were there, for optimism and hopefulness are what later disappeared and could be more deeply noted by their absence.

But what Tommy saw then that he could not name, the undeniable presence that he would see in his mother's eyes later that same night in very different circumstances, (but still could not know or name) was sensuousness. Not an easy trait for a teenage boy to identify, and even harder for a son to acknowledge in his mother.

Mary Lee Patterson now sat stiffly upright, bracing herself for what might come next. She wore her hair pulled back into a tight bun and she tilted her head to one side, better to hear Thomas in the hallway. She stretched her hands flat, palms down on the oak table before her in order to absorb its coolness, as if by that gesture she might steady herself while she waited for Thomas' obviously bad news. Then she stuck out her bottom lip just a bit and gave a little upward puff of breath in an attempt to blow a loose strand of honey-colored hair back from her eyes. She took a deep breath, suddenly smothered by the heaviness of blackened bacon that hung in the air.

Tommy was out of the house in a moment, not wanting to hang around for the inevitable drama and conflict of whatever this problem might be. For he had never–or hardly ever–heard his father react that way, "Lord help us," being unacceptable language in a moment of stress. For his father, times of stress were simply times of problem solving. His father's words 'Keep a clear head, gather the facts, and act prudently' slowed Tommy down just a little as he hurried to the car.

Tommy was determined to remain neutral, not for any reasons of loyalty to one or the other of his parents or for deeply held values of right and wrong. He was determined, however, to do anything, agree to anything not to jeopardize his tenuous and always retractable right to drive the Ford sedan that at that moment was parked in its usual place on the street in front of their house. For he drove that car, he knew, by the luck of living in a small East Texas town. There, the blessing of having a "hardship" driver's license was not hard to come by at fourteen unless you were a known hellion, which Tommy wasn't, but made even easier if you had a father, as he did, who was the most prominent lawyer in town.

The car started on the third try, and Tommy sat there pumping the accelerator enough to feed the sluggish engine without, he hoped, flooding it. He stared straight ahead, down the street of small, mostly frame houses, not daring to turn towards his own house. He was afraid that his mother might have escaped to the wraparound front porch, her bathrobe clutched tight at her throat, and would be frantically trying to wave him down, trying to draw him back into the turmoil of whatever events might be unfolding.

He squinted into the sun, already working its way up and through the pecan trees that lined the street, and eased the car away from the curb. He did catch a glimpse of Odie Mae Harwood rocking on her front porch and he felt vaguely guilty, as if she were passing judgment on him for leaving the turbulence of his house.

By the time he hit second gear Tommy felt buoyant, the confines and subtle battles of family fading quickly behind him. He had escaped their churn and roil, and for the morning, at least, he was on his own.

The car, a 1939 Ford, was the Pattersons' second and not-too-reliable car (a brass-handled set of jumper cables had become a part of the Ford's permanent equipment). But, when the car started, it ran fine, certainly fine enough to carry Tommy the six blocks from the Patterson house into the center of Cottonwood, where today on the courthouse square the Old Fiddlers' Contest would be held.

Tommy washed the car almost every Saturday, dragging a hose from the side of the house. He scrubbed the white walls with soap and a stiff bristle brush and later wiped the car down with a soft chamois. Despite a few nicks here and there, the black sedan looked sharp.

The night before, Tommy's mother had cautioned him. "Now, Tommy," she had whispered as if her words carried unusual and dramatic import, "don't park on the courthouse square in the morning. I know it will be early, and things won't have started then, but when the crowds pour in you will never get out of there. And I will need the Ford in the afternoon for some errands–some important errands." Then she went on to what was really on her mind. "And it's fine to help Gene and his dad set up their stand, but, you know, your father wants you to be careful who your friends are. Sometimes those we spend too much time with will pull us down."

"But Mr. Holley's okay," Tommy had answered. "He's a lot of fun, and Gene's my best friend."

"Just be open to all possibilities," Mary Lee cautioned. "Your father and I want you to lead a rich and full life. We may live in this insignificant town in Texas–that is my cross to bear–but we all can rise above our surroundings. Just look at what your father has done."

She just doesn't understand, Tommy thought as he pulled around the downtown square and parked nose-in out front of the Farmers & Merchants Bank. But she was right about one thing, he couldn't park here too long; before noon the country folks would come flocking in for the festivities, staking out their places on the courthouse lawn with quilts and folding chairs. The women would pass around platters of fried chicken and enameled bowls of black-eyed peas and paper cups of sweet iced tea. And not long after that the fiddlers and pickers and singers and yodelers would take over the stage that was at this very moment being built on a section of the smooth, worn, red brick street. Now the stage appeared to be only a skeleton of yellow pine planks, but before long the half-dozen men who clambered around it would have the flooring in place, and long stretches of corrugated tin would shade the stage before the sun was high. The workers' hammering and sawing and wisecracks already filled the morning air.

Tommy wandered the sidewalk, which was a couple of steps higher than the street, and kept his eye out for his friend Gene Holley. Tommy had agreed to help Gene and his dad unload their portable grill, a giant contraption that Oran Holley had designed and built. He fired the grill with hickory limbs and charcoal, and an ingenious series of belts and gears kept the wieners and hamburger patties moving in a circular pattern that assured even cooking. It was a wonder to Tommy, the way it could handle hundreds of hot dogs and hamburgers a day.

At the time, Tommy thought Gene's dad was terrific, a quick and wiry fellow who had picked up a ton of smarts traveling as a young man with the Al G. Barnes Circus. Rumor had it that when he was a boy he had jumped from the top of a barn with a Rhode Island Red hen under each arm, convinced that together the three of them could fly.

The glamour of the circus wore off for Oran Holley years before when he had witnessed a renegade elephant named Black Diamond kill a woman during a downtown parade over i n Corsicana.

But Oran Holley could still walk on his hands and might do so today if he thought it would attract a crowd of hot dog customers.

Tommy glanced at the clock on the brick-and-sandstone courthouse. Eight-thirty. He wandered back east, shielding his eyes from the rising sun, thinking he would stand on the corner and watch for Mr. Holley's pickup and trailer.

As he passed the B & B Café, a group of three men pushed their way out of the grease-smeared plate glass door and onto the sidewalk. "Not as damned smart as he thinks," one of the men said. Tommy recognized them; he knew almost everyone in town–at least all of the white folks who lived south of the railroad tracks that divided Cottonwood. The one who had just spoken was Vernon Paroline, the only car dealer in Cottonwood, who always cruised around town showing off the latest model Fords. He had sold Thomas Patterson the used Ford that Tommy drove.

Tommy knew the second man only as the owner of the tomato shed over next to the railroad tracks, which, before long, would be packing tomatoes and peas twenty-four hours a day. The third man, Joe Mack Green, towered over both of the others. He was Cottonwood High School's head football coach, a man with a reputation for running his players through a belt line every time they lost a game. The words the three men bandied around ran together and made no sense to Tommy.

"What'll they do now?"

"Aw, it would have been double jeopardy, anyway."

"Scot free and guilty as sin."

"The hell, I say. The hell with the law. The hell with lawyers."

"Right is right, and wrong is wrong."

"Yeah, the damned lawyers are the problem."

All of this floated around Tommy nonsensically, until Joe Mack Green cursed. "Damn him," the big man said. "Damn that Patterson!" Those words jarred Tommy alert.

Then the car dealer spotted Tommy and nudged Joe Mack Green. Coach Green glanced at Tommy. "I don't give a flying fart," he said. Coach Green had guided the Cottonwood Cougars to the regional football playoffs the year before and now was fearless, a town hero who could do no wrong.

The three men eyed Tommy until he had made his way past the café and on to the corner where he waited, watching for his friend, not daring to look back. ❖

Chapter Two

More than a year before, in the early spring of 1947, Thomas Patterson had achieved some notoriety by successfully defending in court a local man, a Negro by the name of Chester Carroll. A sixteen-year old white girl, Corrine Abernathy, claimed to have been attacked–dragged into a thicket of post oak brush and raped–while she was walking the half mile back to her family's farm from Jensen's crossroads store, out near Sand Flats.

It was dusk when the alleged attack occurred, and the assailant had surprised her from behind and forced a burlap tow sack over her head. Despite the semi-darkness of the evening, the quickness of the attack, and the use of the tow sack, Corrine claimed she had gotten a glimpse of her assailant. It was a "colored man," she said, in his twenties, someone who seemed familiar. A local, a man she could without doubt identify. Within a week Chester Carroll was in the county jail, accused of rape.

The county judge pulled a name, Thomas Patterson, from the pool of a half-dozen lawyers who practiced in the county in order to provide the poor man at least the pretense of a defense.

Twenty or thirty years earlier, before the war, a trial in this part of Texas would have been the formality before the hanging, and little notice would have been taken of it–at least not in the white community. But the times had changed and Chester Carroll was different. He had served three years in the European theater, was wounded in the Battle of the Bulge, and came back to Cottonwood with some degree of respect–as much as the white citizens of the town could grant to a Negro man.

Thomas Patterson did not welcome the unpopular task of defending Chester, for already he had ambitions–political ambitions–and a timetable for arriving precisely where he felt his destiny inexorably lay.

"You can turn them down," Mary Lee had counseled him one evening while the decision was still up in the air. "Henry Aldrich," the last decent radio program, had ended at nine, and Tommy had taken a second slice of coconut pie and retreated to his bedroom.

Thomas and Mary Lee moved out to the screened-in back porch, for it was a pleasant spring night. Mary Lee rocked gently in a porch swing while they talked, the squeak of the swing competing with the evening's cicadas and crickets. Thomas settled into a canvas lawn chair. It was dark except for a rectangle of light from the kitchen.

"Yes," Thomas finally responded. "I can turn them down. That is my option." But it was not his option, he knew. That had disappeared many years before.

As a boy Thomas had worked in his father's drug store, out on Oak Lawn, at the northern edge of Dallas. He mostly sprinkled the wooden floors with treated sawdust that held the dust down and swept the store a couple of times a day. Other than that he bicycled prescriptions and over-the- counter remedies to mostly old ladies in the neighborhood.

One day, waiting for his father to fill a prescription, he had sat at one of the marble-top tables and sipped a cherry limeade. A salesman, squat, with round glasses and tufts of hair in his ears, joined the young Thomas. He flopped his valise on the floor and stared up at the ceiling fan, fanning himself with his hat. Salesmen always stopped by, and usually had to wait to see the pharmacist, for business at Patterson's Drug Store was thriving.

This salesman stuck his meaty hand across the table and grunted his name. Thomas shook hands, knowing at once that he had forgotten to grip the way his father had instructed him. The salesman looked around, then reached into the valise and brought out a folder with SAMPLES written across it. He slid the folder across the table and grinned.

The folder contained postcards from Paris, showgirls with long legs and chubby behinds posed in provocative, teasing ways. Thomas shook his head, and glanced back at the high counter where he could see his father's head." Go on, go on," the man said. "You don't care for the girls, then check these out." He reached across the table and flipped the cards until he came to the section he wanted. He nodded. "These are big sellers. Your daddy needs a rack of these. Maybe in the back if there's too many do-gooders around here."

The postcards were made from photographs taken over the past ten years–the dates and places stenciled in the upper left hand corners–of lynchings. Negro men, some of them not more than teenagers, with hands bound behind their backs and ropes around their necks, hung from scaffolding on town squares and from tree limbs in dense woods. Some hung from bridge railings, their feet dangling just above murky rivers. Some of their bodies were burned, and in a couple of them blood streamed down their thighs from vacant groins. In all of the photographs the onlookers grinned into the camera, as if they were at county fairs instead of lynchings.

Behind the lunch counter the Negro cook flipped a grilled cheese sandwich and the pungent smell of burnt cheese filled the store. Thomas felt as if he might throw up. He was ashamed to be fascinated by it all and later wished he had done something, said something.

But he didn't want his father to know he had gawked at the grotesque postcards, or even at the French showgirls. And if he had said anything the salesman might have caused a ruckus, and his daddy would find out, would worry that his son had a deviant side. And Thomas couldn't bear to disappoint him. Thomas could have shoved the cards back across the table to the sweating salesman. But he didn't, and flipped through them one by one. His father dinged a bell on the counter, and Tommy leapt up and made his escape, carrying his guilt and his anger with him.

❖❖❖

"That Chester Carroll is surely guilty," Mary Lee went on, drawing Thomas back onto their back porch. "Are you listening?" Thomas nodded.

"And losing a court case–even one as stacked against you as this–will be a blemish on your record."

Mary Lee dragged the soles of her loafers until the swing rocked to a stop. "Do you think Tommy is all right? You know, going to his room this early. Do you think he's–well, started being interested in, well, you know, girls and things?"

"Homework," Thomas said. "He said he had some homework." He took a sip from the iced tea glass that rested on the floor beside him, and tried to shake those old images from his mind. Maybe he should tell Mary Lee. Then, perhaps, she would understand why he couldn't turn Chester Carroll down.

"It is not your business, Mary Lee, to ask such questions about our son. That is a father's business. And if he starts to go blind I will talk to him. But not before."

Mary Lee laughed, and kicked the swing into motion again. "I just wondered," she said. "How old were you when, well, you know."

Thomas sat straight up. "This Carroll case. I think I will take it on. And despite what you think, by golly, I just might win it." He pushed up from the chair and stood there a moment, staring out into the darkness. "There's still plenty of life, plenty of drive in here." He touched his finger to his chest. He turned towards her, waiting, hoping that Mary Lee would decode his message, but the reference to his virility was much too subtle.

Mary Lee began to swing again, pushing off the wooden floor with her toe to keep her momentum going.

"It's a mistake," she said. "I still say you should stay away from defending nigras. But, I guess no great harm will come of it."

Without another word Thomas stepped outside, easing the screen door shut behind him. There was a concrete bench under a pecan tree. Maybe he would sit there for a while, alone, and think things through. Maybe Mary Lee would turn towards him later when he joined her in bed. Or maybe she would already be asleep, as usual. Sadly, he hardly cared.

So Thomas Patterson, as a future public servant (his ambitions were moderate then–county judge or county attorney seemed lofty goals), took on the case with dedication and diligence.

Right off he recognized Chester Carroll's intelligence and appreciated his sincerity. The Negro man had been "still hunting" for squirrels that afternoon, he claimed, an effort to augment his small monthly disability check with fresh game. Even to hunt, to fire his .22 rifle at a squirrel was a difficult and awkward task for Chester Carroll, for in the last year of the war a German bullet had shattered and rendered his left elbow useless. The afternoon in question he hunted alone, admittedly trespassing onto a wooded tract of land that coincidentally lay not two miles from where the girl purportedly was attacked.

On the witness stand, Corrine identified Chester Carroll as her assailant, "That's the nigger," she sobbed. The packed courtroom gasped, but Thomas retained his calm demeanor through an intense and thorough cross examination.

"So, young lady," Thomas began. "Describe what happened that evening." He spoke not so much to Corrine, but instead faced the jury and the packed court room.

"This man," she said, pointing at Chester Carroll. "He came up behind me and just as I turned around, he shoved a gunny sack over my head."

"A gunny sack?"

"You know," she said. "It smelled sweet, like horse and mule feed."

"A lot of dust from the feed was still in the sack?" Thomas asked. "So that you could smell its sweetness?"

Corrine shrugged. "I guess."

"And did this dust get in your eyes? Did the dust in your eyes make it hard to see?"

"I couldn't see through the bag, anyway," she said.

"And then?"

"That man grabbed me, hard, and dragged me off to the woods. And then . . ."

"Did he wrap his arms around you?" Thomas asked. "Both arms?"

"He grabbed me and held me, so I guess he did."

Thomas turned to Chester Carroll and asked him to stand. "Will you remove your suit coat, please?"

"Yes sir," Chester answered, his intonation of voice that of a military man. He struggled a little, but in a moment held out his coat and the bailiff took it. He wore a short sleeve shirt, thin from many washings.

"Now," Thomas instructed, "hold your arms out, like this." And Thomas extended his arms straight from his side. A woman in the jury shifted forward in her seat.

"Now," Thomas directed, "bend your arms like this." Thomas bent his arms into a circle so that the ends of his fingers touched.

Chester shook his head.

"Go ahead," Thomas said. "Bend your arms like this."

"I can't sir," Chester said. He stared at the marble floor while he spoke, his voice now soft, as if it reluctantly carried his shame.

"Why not?" Thomas asked.

"Steel rod in this one, sir." He lifted his rigid left arm straight out from his side, and Thomas shook his head. "From the war. Is that not correct, Mr. Carroll?"

Chester nodded.

Thomas turned to Corrine. "And this man, with one functioning arm, grabbed and held you?" He shook his head. "Astounding," Thomas said. "In fact, unbelievable." Then he turned to the judge and nodded, and returned to his seat.

At that, the congregation of the Saving Grace Baptist Church–Chester's church–from their places in the colored-only balcony of the court room let loose a series of "Praise the Lords" that had the bailiff on his feet.

All along Thomas considered Corrine Abernathy's story an unlikely fabrication. "She's a flibbertigibbet, a scatter-brain," Thomas had early on confided to Mary Lee in the privacy of their bedroom. "And she does have a dubious reputation around town, as you probably know, both for rectitude and the moral ground on which she stands."

"Or lies," Mary Lee added.

In his closing argument, Thomas cast doubt upon Corrine Abernathy's character, hinting at her well known "flirtatious" nature, and her "penchant for hyperbole." A man in overalls started to rise from the audience, and Thomas heard–or thought he heard–"bastard" muttered. But the bailiff stepped towards him, and the man–who Thomas knew without looking must be Edd Abernathy, Corrine's father–slumped back down on the bench.

Then Thomas appealed to the jury's sense of fairness, an admirable plea for them "not to go down that old and bloody path where justice is meted out in the name of hatred and racism." For everyone knew the stories of Negro men castrated or burned alive or hung for so minor an offense as flirting with a white woman.

As it turned out, Thomas' righteous fervor and Chester's exemplary war record swayed a couple of ex-GIs on the jury to lead the way to acquittal, and Chester Carroll was a free man.

Thomas did receive more than a few hate letters, and one early morning phone call of "Wake up, nigger lover" prompted Thomas to sleep with a loaded 12-gauge shotgun on the floor next to the bed for several weeks. He suspected that the caller was Corrine Abernathy's daddy, and would have requested a restraining order if only he had a sliver of proof.

The *Tyler Morning Telegraph* praised the verdict–along with Thomas' "leadership in establishing a new moral high ground in East Texas"–and the state Democratic machine took notice.

Coke Stevenson kept his conservative silence, but Governor Jester forwarded a handwritten note of middling approval, and an aide to Lyndon Johnson sent a typed note to Thomas that offered the congressman's congratulations, while withholding any direct, quotable praise.

Thomas Patterson emerged as the party's fresh face, fresh voice, someone who might pull the local populace more in line with the larger currents of change that had begun to emerge across the nation.

There were late-night meetings in Thomas' law office, rambling drives through the countryside in cigar smoke-filled sedans. The state district judgeship "seems a little ambitious," he told Mary Lee one night. He had come in late from another secretive "exploration of possibilities" meeting. Mary Lee was propped up in bed, studying a Texas real estate rules and regulations booklet. She had been threatening for months to get her real estate license.

"Maybe county attorney for a start." Thomas unbuttoned his shirt and stepped out of his trousers. "Robert Newsome has done a good job, but a rumor is going around–one that needs to be substantiated, of course–that he will retire at the end of his term."

Mary Lee dropped the booklet to her lap. "Retire? More than likely drop dead on the courthouse steps. He's an old drunk, Thomas. You and I know it. All of Shawnee County knows it. Are those the footsteps you want to follow in?" She sighed. "Where is your ambition? Your daring?"

"I have both sufficient ambition and daring," Thomas said. He slipped off his shirt and folded it carefully before dropping it into the laundry hamper inside the closet. He was down to his knee-high blue socks, his red and white striped boxer shorts, and his undershirt. He pulled his pajamas from an oak chest of drawers.

"You look silly like that," Mary Lee said, "in your shorts and knee socks." She started to giggle.

Thomas carried his folded pajamas into the bathroom. Yes, he probably did look silly in his knee socks and shorts, but Mary Lee looked silly with bobby-pinned ringlets in her hair. He slipped on his pajamas.

Mary Lee was back into her booklet. Thomas eased down on the edge of the bed. He would tell her how he felt, that when she made those demeaning remarks it hurt his feelings and damaged his dignity. If he was to become a state district judge, then he would need the support–and respect–of his family.

Mary Lee looked up. "Why would a sample question ask, 'How many members are on the state real estate board?' What in the world does knowing that have to do with being a competent and qualified real estate broker?"

Thomas ignored her. Mary Lee would have to raise herself to a place of composed self-restraint. Wives of state district judges don't say everything that flits through their heads. There was a necessary decorum that . . .

And then Mary Lee clicked off the bedside lamp. Thomas heard a loud whack as his wife plumped her pillow, and then the squirming and what he took to be a melancholy sigh as she settled into bed. He sat there for a long time, the only noise the ticking of the alarm clock on the dresser. That, and the soft exhalations of Mary Lee's deep and contented sleep.

Daring? Ambitious? Thomas would show them all. Especially Mary Lee. State District Judge Thomas Patterson, he thought. Then he repeated it, this time whispering those same words, hoping they might somehow mingle with Mary Lee's dreams. ❖

Chapter Three

Thomas Patterson felt sick. Not just emotionally sick or metaphorically sick, but physically, in the deepest center of his gut, sick. He waved off Mary Lee, ignored her questions about the early morning telephone call with a shake of his head as he hurried to the bathroom, just barely making it before the lumpy eggs and charred bacon and burnt and scraped toast all rushed forth, as if propelled by some dark demon that had entered into the core of Thomas' very body and soul.

When her husband had exclaimed into the telephone, "Lord, help us all," a few moments before, Mary Lee had gasped, thinking that someone had died, perhaps Thomas' widowed mother who lived in Dallas. But that would have elicited a different response from her husband, a solemn, yet controlled reaction. Perhaps one tinged with an element of relief that only Mary Lee would discern. No, it was not his mother.

Oh! Perhaps another war had broken out, and Tommy, just four years short of enlistment age, would die on foreign soil or come home an amputee or deranged from some new trench poison that even the most advanced gas masks couldn't filter out. Oh, my God!

Mary Lee followed Thomas to the bathroom and waited by the door, listening. As she leaned against the smooth doorframe, she caught herself nervously and inappropriately humming "The Gypsy," her favorite song of the past year. And in her mind she could see a gypsy woman wearing a red scarf and sitting in a horse-pulled wagon in some strange and foreign country. The gypsy's eyes glistened with faraway dreaminess, as if she truly was able to peer into the future and predict all sorts of exotic events.

Mary Lee began to sing, really whisper, the lyrics, in spite of her best intentions and her worry. And again inappropriately–what was wrong with her? –she whirled away from the door in a slow and sultry dance.

When at last the commode flushed, gurgled, and slowly refilled, and after the lavatory faucet ran and ran (it seemed like forever to Mary Lee), Thomas emerged, his shirt and tie untouched by the ordeal, his face pale, washed-out, but composed. He moved to the bed and sat, smoothing the wrinkles in the bedspread with one hand.

"What is it?" Mary Lee asked. "Are you all right? Who in the world was that on the phone? Oh, talk to me! Dammit! Please talk to me!"

At the "Dammit!" Thomas cut his eyes up at Mary Lee for just a moment. Then he held up his hand, asking for silence. "Chester Carroll is dead," he said, his voice calm and level.

"Oh," Mary Lee said, relieved that none of the scenarios that had continued to flicker through her mind were true. Then she knew. Or she thought she knew. "Oh, my God! He's been killed, murdered by the Klan!" And she glanced at the bedroom door, wondering if whoever had murdered Chester Carroll might also want to kill his lawyer. And maybe the wife of his lawyer.

"Chester Carroll had been sick," Thomas continued, ignoring Mary Lee's theatrics. "I knew that." He had run into the Reverend William Isaacs at the post office one morning a few months back, and the good Reverend, who shepherded the flock at Saving Grace Baptist Church, had lamented Chester's complications from a blood disorder. "A curse upon God's children of color," the reverend had said with a shake of his head. A bout of kidney malfunctions followed by a mild stroke had necessitated Chester's long stay in the veterans' hospital over in Waco. "It has him down in the dumps," the reverend had said, this report of a former client's health of little concern to Thomas at the time.

"No," Thomas now calmly said. "He was not murdered. He killed himself."

Mary Lee was puzzled. A sad event. Yes. But why Thomas' reaction? Why all the trauma? She started to ask, but he cut her off.

"Let me finish," he said. He stepped into the bathroom again and unwound a length of tissue paper that he carefully folded on the seams. He dabbed at the perspiration on his forehead and above his lip before moving back to where his wife waited. He eased back down on the edge of the bed again.

"The man was sick," Thomas said. He almost had said, "The *poor* man was sick," but caught himself, for he felt no sympathy whatsoever for Chester Carroll. "Yes, he was sick, with this sickle cell disease, or something, a blood problem of some kind. And his prospects were not good. A young man, not yet thirty, but with one useless arm, and then this disease. No, his prospects were not good at all. Especially living with all of that guilt."

"What in the world are you talking about, Thomas Patterson? Can't you please, please, please get to the point?" Mary Lee began to pace the room, and then once again she had the desire to dance, to move to the gypsy song that would not leave her alone. She threw up her arms in despair, but moved with the slightest of twirls as she did so.

The phone rang in the hallway. It jolted Mary Lee. "Don't answer it," Thomas said. After nine rings it stopped. "It will ring again," he sighed. "Again and again."

Then Thomas held out both his hands, palms turned up, as if he carried something fragile. "So he shot himself. With his old .22. I'm surprised it would even kill him. But it did." Thomas took a deep breath. "Chester left a note behind for Reverend Isaacs, with instructions for him to go to his mother to ask for her forgiveness . . . and so on." With that he looked hard at Mary Lee, hard enough to frighten her. "But, more importantly, and more disastrous–for me, for us–he also asked the reverend to deliver to Robert Newsome, the county attorney–who, as you know, had failed to convict Chester of the assault and rape of Corrine Abernathy–asked him to deliver his handwritten admission of guilt."

"Oh, my God!" Mary Lee sank down on the bed beside her husband. "What will you do now?"

Thomas gave an uncharacteristic shrug. He wanted Mary Lee to touch him, to give him comfort in some way. Instead she suddenly stood and moved–almost seemed to twirl–away from him.

So, as usual, Thomas would collect himself, order his thoughts, and take appropriate and deliberate action. Lawyers represented guilty parties all of the time. It happened in every criminal case. It was a lawyer's duty to exert all of his skills in representing the accused to the best of his ability.

But this was different, and Thomas knew it. For some would say (had, in fact, said after the trial) that he had deliberately confused poor Corrine and had twisted and turned her own truthful testimony to the advantage of a colored man now known to be guilty.

The telephone rang again. This time Thomas rose from the bed and with quick, determined strides made his way past Mary Lee to the hallway, where, with some trepidation, he lifted the receiver. It was one of those faceless aides to Governor Jester. "As a precaution," the man said, with no preliminaries at all, "and due to the unfortunate developments of yesterday, the governor thinks it might be more appropriate for his old friend, Buddy Melton, to give the introductory remarks to open the Old Fiddlers' contest."

Thomas nodded and said, "I see."

"The governor wants me to assure you that"–and for a moment or two Thomas could only pick up a muffled voice on the other end of the line–"assure you that he will be in contact with you at a later date, but not today, and that"–again a pause and the muffled voice–"that he appreciates your support, and so on."

And so on? Thomas thought. He softly placed the telephone back in its cradle. By then Mary Lee was at his side.

"It appears I will have some free time today. Buddy Melton will be introducing the governor. Can you believe it?" he asked.

Buddy Melton was an old-time political crony from Smith County, a man who had made his only mark, and that a minor one, twenty years earlier when he stomped out of the National Democratic Convention when Al Smith won the party's nomination. The *Houston Post* carried Buddy Melton's comments: "When that Smith fellow got the nomination and his Yankee supporters jammed the aisles, marching with their banners, full of their jabber, I looked around at the whole bunch of them and wondered where were all the Americans."

Later, Buddy Melton proposed the theory that the utility poles springing up all over the rural areas of the state were part of a Catholic plot to spread the symbol of the cross throughout Texas.

"An old reprobate, a dinosaur," Mary Lee said. "When the governor could have . . . "

"Please," Thomas said. "A little time, a little quiet will put this all in perspective." He began to pace the floor, his leather heels clicking across the pine-planked floor. "Forget the Old Fiddlers' Contest, and forget the governor–for now. The congressman, Lyndon Johnson, will show up late this afternoon. Perhaps we will go to the barbecue for him tonight at the country club. The governor won't be there, and old Buddy Melton is a Coke Stevenson man. Let me see what I can do, see if the congressman might appreciate my support."

Mary Lee cocked her head to one side. "Well, the barbecue tonight might be fine, if you don't mind what people will be saying. Oh, I don't know if I can stand it. You were only doing your job. That terrible man. How could he have lied to you? Couldn't you tell that Chester Carroll was not telling you the truth?"

"Don't even say that, Mary Lee." Thomas turned pale once more, and Mary Lee was afraid that he might race to the bathroom again. "I don't have a crystal ball." Thomas slumped down on the edge of the bed. "Am I a failure? Have all of my work and my ambition and my dreams come to nothing? What will become of me?"

You? Mary Lee thought, but said nothing. She touched his arm, a wifely touch of solace, of support, as she saw it. But she felt angry and hurt and was now unsure about a future–her future–that had held so much promise. Perhaps Byron Bostick would not call her, and her career in real estate would be jeopardized, damaged before it had even begun. "Oh," she said, her mind jumping back and forth, out of her control, it seemed.

"But you can't support Congressman Johnson. Just this morning you said . . . "

"I quite clearly remember what I said–that I was officially neutral."

"And that Lyndon Johnson didn't have–as I remember you distinctly saying–'a ghost of a chance.' Your very words."

Thomas sighed. "Perhaps you're right. The man has no chance. A lot of effort–and risk–on my part to bet on a long shot candidate. And everyone who matters will be at the reception. Maybe we shouldn't go at all. Maybe staying out of sight would be best. No, don't plan on going this evening." Thomas threw up his hands in exasperation, a gesture so unlike him that it alarmed Mary Lee. "I need some time–some time alone–to think, to figure this out."

The telephone rang again. "Mary Lee, will you please get that? And remember. We will be cool and in control; our comments will be neutral and unemotional. And I am not here. Absolutely not here." ❖

Chapter Four

By noon the courthouse square was packed. Tommy had worked the last two hours for Oran Holley and eaten his fill of free hot dogs loaded down with mustard and chili and onions. He gave Gene a wave and said he would see him later; the novelty of mashing hamburger patties flat on the hot grill with a heavy spatula had soon run its course. With a wink and a grin, Mr. Holley pressed a quarter into Tommy's hand.

His mother had been right. The Ford was blocked in by an ice delivery truck, and a string of sawhorses cut across the south side of the square. But it didn't matter. His mother had said she would need the car "in the afternoon," an expression that Tommy saw as loaded with flexibility. And he didn't want to go home, because something was wrong–he knew that–and he tried to piece together the phone call that so upset his father and how it connected with Coach Joe Mack Green's blurting out, "That damned Patterson." He would make the connection, or someone would make it for him–whether he liked it or not. But his mother would be upset, and Tommy didn't want to hear her go on and on. He would stay put. The car being blocked in was a welcome excuse.

He crossed to the east side of the square, making his way past the stage, which was now complete. A man in a western hat messed with the sound system, and a couple of fiddlers in the shade of the stage rehearsed "Old Shep." Tommy moved on to the Dixie Theater and stopped for a minute to check the poster out front. "Dead Man's Gold," with Lash LaRue would be on at two and four. A movie might be a good escape, a way to hide out for a couple of hours. He fingered the quarter in his pocket. A little earlier, while he was turning hamburger patties, he had spotted Zoette Acton, a girl who had moved into town with her family and showed up in Tommy's eighth grade class in April. Zoette was different, a dark-skinned girl with deep chocolate eyes and black hair. Today she wore white shorts, lemon-colored string sandals, and a scooped-neck blouse. When she bent over to pull a Grapette out of the icy tub at the next stand, Tommy saw the old fellow behind the double-plank counter stop for a moment, his eyes fixed on whatever forbidden sight he had spotted down her blouse. Tommy would have given anything to have been there in that old man's place.

Zoette's family had wandered into town pulling a two-wheeled, round-fronted green trailer that they parked on a vacant patch of ground a couple of miles out the Dallas highway. There, a candy factory had churned out fudge and pralines before the war, but sugar rationing had forced it to shut down. Zoette's father set up a store, of sorts, in the front office of the old place and sold used furniture that he bought, repaired, and painted. Zoette's mother–a woman who seemed young enough to be her sister–supposedly could read the future, and for a while a sign out in front of their trailer advertised "CARD and PALM READINGS." The sign mysteriously disappeared one night not many days after the pastor of the Central Baptist Church, in a letter to the editor of the *Cottonwood Clarion*, protested that the woman's claims of "magic" made her a "servant of the devil."

Tommy dismissed it all as grown-up bickering, but his mother had seemed fascinated by their exoticism. "Is it any weirder than what the Catholics do?" she asked Thomas one evening at dinner, the day after news of the stolen sign had made the local paper. "With all of their incense and candles and Latin mumbling?" Thomas never looked up, but relentlessly sawed a pork chop into smaller and smaller pieces. "Hocus-pocus," he finally said. "It's all hocus-pocus." Thomas claimed to be a "progressive" Methodist, one who did not allow the concerns of the church to disrupt the orderliness of his life.

Tommy hoped Zoette was now still in town and he searched over the gathering crowd–the town men in slacks and white shirts and snappy straw hats worn at rakish angles, and country men in overalls and coarse straw work hats, their women in paisley flour-sack dresses. Back the other way, Early Caldwell, "The Tamale King," wearing a long white apron and a tall white toque, pulled a bundle of tamales from a cast iron pot that sat in the shade of his Model A. The old Negro man nodded to a stocky lady while he wrapped a stack of tamales in a layer of newspaper and secured them with a few quick circles of twine. On down the street, three older boys from high school leaned against a shiny Chevy pickup. They seemed to be staring at Tommy, so he quickly looked away. But there was no Zoette. Maybe he would run into her later, somewhere around the square. Maybe he would ask her to go see "Dead Man's Gold," and maybe, in the dark, he would hold her hand. And who could know what else, with a girl like Zoette? Tommy took a deep breath. He would need to practice what he would say, how he would ask her. It wouldn't be easy.

Just after noon the master of ceremonies, a Cottonwood insurance agent who also headed up a local three-man band, climbed onto the stage to announce the order of the day's competition. The over-sixty fiddlers would start things off, but nothing would begin until Governor Jester's kickoff speech at one. "And," the insurance man continued, "be assured that the governor has arrived, is at this moment in his room across the way," and he gestured towards the Deen Hotel, a two-story brick building on the corner where Cottonwood's two highways crisscrossed.

Tommy worked his way back through the crowd that already had bunched up around the elevated stage. The emcee worked to coax a high screech out of the P.A. system, and below the stage a cacophony of tuning began to rise with increasing urgency.

Back at Oran Holley's hamburger stand Gene was taking a break, sitting on the running board of their truck and slowly dropping peanuts one at a time into a bottle of Dr Pepper. Gene looked bushed. He was a stocky kid with freckles and always seemed to have beads of perspiration hovering above his lip. He played center on the junior high football team, and during the season his hair took on the tight-fitting helmet's orange dye and the older boys had tagged him "Pumpkin," a nickname that Gene hated.

Tommy plopped down beside his pal. Gene held out the sack of peanuts. Tommy took a handful. "Too bad about your daddy," Gene said. "Getting in trouble like that. A nigger's not worth it."

"What do you mean? Who said that he was in trouble?" Tommy strained to stay cool, to look nonchalant. He tossed a peanut in the air and tried to catch it in his mouth, but missed.

"Everybody knows. That nigger who raped the Abernathy girl really did do it. Hell, I knew it. My daddy said everybody knew he did it. And now he even confessed it–before he done himself in."

"What do you mean?" Tommy asked. Gene glanced around. "I heard them deputies talkin' about it. They was watchin' out to see if old man Abernathy might show up here today, with a gun or something." Then he went on in a hushed voice, filling Tommy in on the story as best he could.

When Gene had finished, Tommy stood and checked

the clock below the dome of the courthouse. This story meant trouble. "Listen," he said, "I've got to get home. My mom needs the car and she'll be all over me if I'm late."

"Hey," Gene said. "You going to see the helicopter? That Johnson fellow, the one runnin' for senator, he's supposed to light down out at the junior college about four. Man, I'd like to see that. I've never seen a helicopter up close."

Tommy hadn't heard about the helicopter, and it did sound like fun. He and Gene had found the plans for a one-man gyro-copter in a stack of Oran Holley's *Popular Science* magazines and had seriously studied how they could build one. They salvaged a Briggs and Stratton engine from a junk lawn-mower and they scrounged plenty of scrap lumber from a half-finished house down the street. But the propeller and gears stumped them and the idea died. That didn't bother Tommy, because he got woozy just thinking about lifting off more than a dozen feet.

But to see a helicopter up close might inspire him again. If some congressman would fly all over Texas in one, maybe it wasn't so scary after all. That Johnson must be an awful brave man. Or maybe he was a little crazy. Tommy figured he could tell if he saw him up close. His mother would have the Ford, but he could bicycle the few blocks to the college if he had to. If what Gene said about his father was true, then his mom would be having a hissy-fit, and Tommy would need somewhere–anywhere–to go.

"Yeah," Tommy said. "Maybe I'll see you there."

He started to take off, but all of a sudden Oran Holley was next to him, wiping his hands on an apron that almost touched the brick surface of the street. Oran leaned close–he was no more than half a head taller than Tommy–and glanced to his right and left. He spoke to Tommy in a whisper, but with the fiddling from the stage and the hum and murmur and laughter of the crowd, the words almost floated and slipped away.

"Your daddy's a smart man," Oran said. "A lot smarter than me. But folks can be unreasonable, downright mean sometimes. And if you get the chance you might tell Mr. Patterson that my advice is for him to lay low for a while." Oran shrugged. "None of my business, for sure, but I can read a crowd–I've worked them all over the country–and this bunch . . . " He looked away from Tommy and glanced back at his hamburger stand. "I've got to get back." He motioned to Gene, and in a moment they both were back in the stand, lost in a swirl of smoke.

With a wave Tommy took off in a trot, headed for his car. But then he remembered that it was getting close to one and his daddy would be on the Old Fiddlers' stage introducing the governor. He slowed down and worked his way back through the crowd to the courthouse lawn, where he settled down on a patch of grass in the shade of a pecan tree. He went over what Gene had told him. His pal didn't always get his stories straight, and neither did Oran Holley, who, Thomas Patterson had said, was the kind of man "who loved a good story more than he loved the truth."

"Oh, they need all of their small-town gossip and rumors and lies," his mother often said with a dismissive wave of her hand. The wave being her way of defusing some story of a banker secreted off to a drying-out facility in Dallas, or a high school girl suddenly disappearing from town, "visiting her aunt" in Houston for most of nine months.

But this seemed to be more than just another rumor. Tommy wouldn't worry. Not yet. For sure he wouldn't pass along Oran Holley's warning to his daddy. Maybe he would tell his mom, if she wasn't having one of her hysterical fits.

He checked around once more for Zoette, but his heart

was no longer in the hunt, and he stretched back on the grass, finding comfort in being alone. ❖

Chapter Five

When Thomas had announced to Mary Lee that if anyone called, "I am not here. Absolutely not here," he meant it. For only a minute later Thomas folded his suit coat over his arm, pulled his best straw hat down tight over his forehead, and without another word to his startled wife deliberately strode out the front door to his Buick waiting in the narrow garage at the side of the house.

Normally Thomas' sense of worth heightened when he slid into the driver's seat of the Buick. The car, a 1947 two-door Super sedan, with its classic lines and restrained shade of green, proclaimed that its owner was a person of substance. The car established Thomas–in his eyes, at least–as someone formidable, a man to be reckoned with in the jousting for advantage that was, regrettably, an integral element of his profession. Certainly for a man with Thomas' ambitions.

The grill of the Buick gleamed like giant silver teeth, and the car's dramatic sweep–accented by fender skirts that half-covered the rear wheels–gave the impression that the automobile was eager to roar to life. He had bought it new, drove it back from Dallas, already anxious as the odometer relentlessly climbed and the clock on the dash clicked, moving towards the limits of the four thousand mile, ninety day warranty.

Of course, Mary Lee complained about the two doors, how it was a strain and an unnecessary effort for anyone other than Tommy to maneuver into the back seat. But that was nitpicking, Thomas thought. Just another small complaint that

Mary Lee–now habitually, it seemed–compiled and saved in her ever ready resentment file.

An ad he came across in *The Saturday Evening Post* had boasted of the car's "fireball power," but today the Buick seemed sluggish, and Thomas regretted ever buying it. All of that money for something so ephemeral and fleeting as a shiny new car.

He parked behind his office, just a block from the courthouse square, and without looking to the left or to the right–and all the while ignoring the screech of the PA system and the background murmur of the crowd in town–he slipped into the semi-darkness of the building.

The office was well located, an easy walk to the courthouse and the title company, less than a block the other way. The office was originally a house, but Thomas had had the imagination and foresight to purchase it from an estate when the owner died. It was a modest place when he bought it, but he had renovated it quite nicely. He turned the kitchen into an all-purpose storage room; the living room became his secretary's office, with room for a sofa and a couple of chairs for visitors. That left one bedroom to be made into his office and one for a conference room, with a walnut library table and six straight-back matching chairs. Thomas now regretted spending so much on the conference room furniture, but that had been Mary Lee's idea. The bathroom at first appeared problematic, but Mary Lee had the carpenter splice together and then trim a half dozen 1 X 6 tongue-and-groove boards to fit on top of the claw foot bathtub. Mary Lee painted the boards sunny yellow and situated all sorts of potted plants there. She did have a way with decorating, Thomas had to admit.

It annoyed him that Belinda Donohoo, his secretary, ended up with the most spacious office, especially since she was a Seventh Day Adventist, a gangly, high-waisted woman in her thirties would frown over her glasses and shake her head in quiet disapproval if Thomas brought back a bacon and tomato sandwich for lunch from the drug store counter. She wouldn't come in to the office on Saturdays, not even to type a letter, but secretaries with half a lick of sense weren't easy to come by, so Thomas overlooked that.

Thomas' private office, though smaller than Belinda's, was adequate–actually quite impressive. For visitors could not help but notice his two framed degrees on the wall and a letter of appreciation from the Dallas law firm where he had clerked.

Settled at his desk Thomas lost himself in a series of lists, his time-proven way of problem solving: one list of the elements and conditions that created the problem, another list of alternative actions that he could take, and still another set of lists that forecast the possible consequences and weighed each consequence with a formula of his own devising.

But despite his power of concentration, an attribute that he was justly proud of, his mind roamed here and there. Perhaps he should have stayed in Dallas where his family had a reputation of some significance. His father had owned that drugstore for years out on Oak Lawn and, before his stroke and subsequent death two years before, had acquired a second store way out north in a new neighborhood near Mockingbird Lane.

A law practice in Dallas would have been easy to slip into, but Mary Lee and his mother in the same city–even one as large as Dallas–was a guarantee of conflict and turmoil. It seemed that Mary Lee got a perverse sense of pleasure in opposing whatever her mother-in-law valued. And, Thomas would admit, Adelle Patterson could be a difficult and hard-headed woman.

Adelle was a literalist, had learned the splitting of fine hairs in the middle row of the same church for almost sixty years. There was black, and there was white–grudgingly there was white–because Adelle seemingly took pleasure in doom and gloom scenarios. So there was mostly black, and no gray at all. None of this lukewarm business, if you please. Even the Bible warned of that.

Lawyers are born to be lawyers, Thomas knew, law school is only the fine tuning, the refinement of what already was in place. And from Adelle came his lawyerly precision, the ability to grasp the essence of things and ignore all of the mumbo-jumbo in which other less focused minds would flounder.

But holidays, especially, were unbearable, Adelle insisting that everyone–Thomas and Mary Lee and Tommy, and Mary Margaret, Thomas' school teacher sister from Fort Worth, and her too-quiet husband and four bratty kids, and even a pair of bossy aunts–all gather at her Dallas house.

Mary Lee seethed through those holiday gatherings, complaining under her breath to Thomas about the soggy cornbread dressing and the too sweet iced tea and the runny raisin pie. Finally Thomas would retreat to the screened-in back porch and chew on an unlit cigar until the predictable explosion occurred. Then Thomas, put in the untenable position of trying to negotiate peace between the two women, would give up and leave, driving off with Mary Lee and Tommy, loaded down with an unbearable load of guilt. No, Dallas would not have worked out.

But there had been other possibilities, and Thomas felt an odd combination of both shame and yearning when he conjured up his memory of Evelyn Ramsey. Sweet-natured, gentle, and soft-spoken, she worked as a legal secretary in the Dallas office of Banks and Farrell where Thomas clerked the summer before his graduation–and the summer before he married.

He was engaged at the time to Mary Lee, who after two years at North Texas State Teachers' College had moved back home to live with her parents in Tyler, a hundred miles east of

Dallas. There she worked part-time as a receptionist in a local real estate office. Bored, Mary Lee constantly bombarded Thomas with letters that hinted at sensual pleasures soon to come and complaints about nothing to do in a hick town like Tyler.

Lovely, lovely Evelyn Ramsey, now Thomas could see, had carried on a discreet flirtation with him for the months he worked there. But at the time Thomas thought her to be simply friendly and cheerful and so accommodating. In hindsight, he saw that when he approached her with some document to type, she had not gone out of her way to cover her knees with her skirt when she swiveled around in the chair to face him. Or when he stood above her, nodding his approval while she typed, Evelyn never made the slightest movement, not to adjust a wayward strap nor to touch a pucker of her blouse, when she must have known that Thomas all the time furtively eyed the rise and fall of the fullness of her pale skin.

For a moment, an elemental urge, a movement, pulsed in his groin, and he glanced around at the door, both guilty and embarrassed.

On the afternoon he had left his summer job, Evelyn presented him with a gold tie tack, and as he stammered his thanks, she had kissed him lightly on the cheek and squeezed his hand, holding it just a little longer than seemed proper. What would his life have been if he had allowed Evelyn into his world? In place of Mary Lee? With Evelyn's sweetness and calm she would have embraced Adelle, and Thomas would have avoided all of the useless and draining conflict that seemed to accompany their family gatherings.

He shook his head at the thought, trying to weigh the assets and liabilities of peace and probable boredom versus his present life of volatility and–at least earlier–excitement with Mary Lee. Perhaps he would make a series of lists someday and address those possibilities. But he knew he wouldn't. For him it was too late. With a sense of regret that he couldn't shake, he returned to the problems at hand.

An hour or more back into this process–Thomas had lost all sense of time and all connection with the outside world–a tapping on the glass of the rear door jarred him back.

The only light in the office–Venetian blinds tightly covered all of the windows–was from a small lamp on his desk, and Thomas reached to click it off, but he didn't. He waited. He knew that this could be trouble–more trouble. For he was grounded enough in the ways of this small town to know that beneath the idle talk and bantering and teasing that provided the surface social lubrication, there was pettiness and ignorance and even desperation. Too often a bad dog hid under the welcoming front porch of a house.

But this was no bad dog that Thomas found at the back door, rather a couple of well-dressed men with straw hats pulled low over their eyes. Although he had never met Beauford Jester, he recognized the governor right away. Jester's aide, a dough-bellied fellow who appeared to have been stuffed into his suit, pushed the door open when he spotted Thomas and turned the latch when he shut the door behind them.

The governor checked his pocket watch. "I only have a few minutes," he said. His voice was deep and comforting. His demeanor and looks reminded Thomas of the late FDR. The governor did not remove his straw hat, an indication to Thomas that this visit indeed would be brief.

They found seats in the study, surrounded by walls of law books. Thomas closed and pushed to one side a biography of Woodrow Wilson he intended to read. The governor touched the book. "A good man, and a good enough president–if you can overlook that wrongheaded League of Nations." Thomas nodded and waited. Finally the aide started things off. "The circumstances that we find ourselves in today are regrettable." While he talked he fiddled with a cigar. "And the decisions that the governor has been forced to make are difficult. But we want you to know . . ."

"I want you to know," the governor said, dismissing his aide with a wave of his hand, "that I see this as only a temporary setback for you. Actually, I believe this unfortunate turn of events will flush the racists from their cover, and in the long run the people of this state will see that justice–as imperfect as it may be–was legally and constitutionally served. They will see that your motives were pure, your efforts on behalf of the accused–a colored man at that–were exemplary.

"All's well that ends well, the poet said, and I have faith that all will end well." He stopped then and seemed pleased with his well-rehearsed speech. He gestured towards Thomas.

"So this means . . . what? For me?" Thomas pushed back from the conference table. "That I withdraw from the contest for district judge? I filed for the primary election, placed my name on the ballot on May 12. Now I have to meekly withdraw to the sidelines when I have done nothing–and I repeat that–nothing wrong?" He shook his head. "That, my dear sir, would be humiliating."

The governor leaned forward, impatience in his voice. "Right or wrong, my *dear* Mr. Patterson, has nothing to do with this. Politics is the name of the game, and the electorate is fickle. I am merely reading the mood of the people." He stood. "Sometimes we have to place the good of the party and the good of the state of Texas above our own–may I say–more personal needs." The dough-bellied aide smirked and nodded his agreement.

The two men moved to the door. Then the governor turned and offered Thomas his hand, but it was the aide who spoke up. "You do understand, sir." He handed Thomas a card. "Please contact me if you need further clarification." Thomas ignored him.

"You are young," Governor Jester said, the warmth back in his voice. "I would think that in two, at the outside four years, if you are able to repair the damage that has been done . . . Well, I think your prospects will be bright." And with that they slipped out the back door and left Thomas alone, sunk into his own desperate thoughts, surrounded by tablets of his now useless lists.

At one o'clock when Thomas knew that the governor would be on stage in the next block–a place that Thomas should have been–he slipped back out to his Buick and drove home, cutting across the quiet back streets of Cottonwood. He found Mary Lee in their bedroom, still in her bathrobe, sitting at the vanity.

She turned, and in a glance at her husband knew that there would be no good news. But she listened quietly, occasionally moving her head side to side while Thomas haltingly described the governor's visit. "What do we do?" she asked when finally Thomas had finished.

"We have no choice," Thomas said, suddenly energized by what he saw as his one last possibility. "It is a long shot, I admit, but we will go on as if nothing has happened. The governor, thank goodness, will soon leave for Austin. We will fall back on Congressman Johnson." Mary Lee started to object, but he silenced her with his raised hand. "I know what I said earlier, but we have no other option. Johnson will be arriving by helicopter at four or so. I must say that he is somewhat fearless, or perhaps a daredevil and simply foolish. Anyway, later, after all of the campaign folderol, our old friend Robert Newsome will be hosting that gathering at the country club in honor of the man. We were, as you know, invited–before all of this Chester Carroll mess came about. And no one, I am sure, will expect to see us there."

Then Thomas began to pace the room, from closet to bed to door, as if he were trying to triangulate the problem. "But," he went on, "we will surprise them. Yes, we will go–the three of us, our family united as one–and we will partake of the barbecue and listen to the awful music–you may not know that the winning band from today's contest will be there to entertain." He shrugged. "But that does not matter," he said with an affirmative nod. "Because I, my dear, will discuss this unfortunate matter–and my political future–with a man who will not pander to the racists for political gain–the man who may well be the next United States Senator from Texas."

With that he slammed his fist into his palm so hard that Mary Lee rocked back on the stool. She had never seen Thomas so unrestrained. "But I thought you favored Coke Stevenson," she said. "And just this morning you claimed that Congressman Johnson has no chance."

"Yes, I admit I did. But all of this . . . this despicable mess, has cleared my vision. Now I see who the progressives are and I have decided that my future is with them, not with the dinosaurs, the reprobate Dixiecrats. Our fates are intertwined."

Mary Lee suddenly had a vision of Thomas making this very same speech to a crowd of hundreds. She would be on the stage behind him, silently urging him on, not as a stodgy judge's wife, but as an equal, a woman who knows how to dress in the latest–perhaps subdued–fashion and converse intelligently with Thomas' colleagues and constituents alike. And Byron Bostick with his wandering eyes could just keep his boring old real estate business all to his flirty self.

Suddenly she saw Thomas as years younger and she remembered, faintly, the promise she had glimpsed when they first met. Well, her husband could count on her to help.

Mary Lee turned to him. "What should I wear tonight? Something that the future senator from Texas might like?" She laughed then, and so did he, the first time they had laughed in ages.

❖❖❖

For almost an hour Mary Lee tried on dresses from the closet. There weren't that many when you got right down to it. What can a sophisticated woman wear, anyway, to a barbecue and hillbilly band party, when the next senator from Texas would be present, and her husband's entire future perhaps hinged on the impression that she, Mary Lee Patterson, might make on those who had gathered there. Especially on Congressman Johnson.

She wished she knew more about him. She wished she had a new dress. She needed a strategy, some guidance. Her best friend Kate Crowder who ran the Smart Shoppe in town might have an answer. At the very least, Kate might have a new shipment of dresses in from Dallas.

A new dress, yes. But Mary Lee needed more than that. She needed insight and direction and assurance. What to say and do, how to act at the barbecue this evening. She needed a grand plan that would propel the Pattersons back onto the road to success. And she knew that Kate could never provide that.

Where in the world was Tommy? He had better show up soon or there would be real trouble. Thomas now had gone back to his office, carrying a waxed paper wrapped meat loaf sandwich that Mary Lee had hurriedly put together, for his "strategy planning session," he had said, and wouldn't be back until after five.

Mary Lee knew he would be filling a legal pad with lists and weighing this against that, on and on. Just the thought of it drove her crazy. Thomas could be so indecisive. Well, Mary Lee wasn't. She would take charge–of Thomas' future and her own life. But how? And then, at the same time she heard the Ford pull up outside the house, the answer came to her. ❖

Chapter Six

Right at one o'clock, Governor Jester made his way through the crowd that had gathered around the bandstand, and Tommy sat up, wrapping his arms around his knees. From there on the courthouse lawn he would be able to see and hear everything. It would be boring, he was certain, but he did feel a sense of pride that his father would be there for all the town to see.

The master of ceremonies blew softly into the microphone and nodded. He raised his arms for silence and the crowd quieted down. Vendors stopped pulling cold drinks from the tubs, and mothers hushed their children with stern looks and fingers to their lips.

The emcee turned the microphone over to a pudgy man in a too tight cream-colored suit. Thomas Patterson was nowhere in sight. Tommy stood. He could see the four or five men on the stage and he recognized the governor, who waved and nodded at the hushed gathering, from newspaper photographs. The pudgy man went on and on, his words ringing out over the crowd, and finally, to a scattering of applause, the governor took center stage.

The governor glanced down at his notes, as if he had forgotten where he was, or what he had planned to say. But before he could even open his mouth, Coach Joe Mack Green hopped up on the tailgate of a nearby pickup. He took off his Cougar baseball cap and waved it around. "Mr. Governor," he said. "With all due respect. Before you get all started here, would you mind answering one question."

In addition to his coaching, Joe Mack Green taught a senior civics class each semester. He considered himself to be Cottonwood High School's expert-in-residence not only on pulling guards in the single wing formation, but the town's authority on the machinations of government and politics. "This question is not just for me," he said, his voice booming, almost exploding from deep in his chest, "but I figure I'm speaking for the whole bunch of us."

The crowd mostly hooted and hollered in support of the coach, but there were a few hisses. A chant broke out spontaneously, "Hey, hey what-a-ya-say, Cougars, Cougars all the way!"

Coach Green lifted his arms for silence. "Now this is serious folks."

"As serious as football?" some joker hollered out, and the crowd laughed. But when Coach Green frowned they got quiet. "This is truly serious folks. Dead serious." He turned back to the governor, who wore a forced smile while he waited.

"My question is this," Coach Green continued. "When the courts–and the lawyers especially–don't know right from wrong. Or even worse, when they do know right from wrong, but still let colored boys terrorize and attack our women, and get away with it, isn't it time for the people to take charge, to find the way for justice all on their own?" The crowd murmured their approval, waiting for the governor to respond.

Beauford Jester had not become governor by taking sides in controversial situations. His political success was born in compromise, the masterful manipulating of opposing points of view for his own benefit.

So he ignored the coach's question at first, starting out his speech instead with an anecdote, relating how this Old Fiddlers' Contest was dear to his heart, and how indeed, he had chosen the Pioneer Fiddle Band to entertain at his inauguration celebration back in January of 1947. "Love that old-timey fiddle music," he said, and the crowd came alive with their approval.

The governor paused then, and turned to face Coach Green. He welcomed the question, he said, drawing on his politically astute and commanding manner, for the governor was an imposing figure, distinguished in appearance and formidable in size. He started in on a series of rhetorical questions and hypothetical situations that before long left Coach Joe Mack Green slack-jawed and disoriented, and the crowd in a state of silent confusion.

But by then Tommy was racing back to his car, dodging this and sidestepping that, and for a moment he forgot about his father and his problems, and transported himself to next fall when he would call upon his quickness and speed as a freshman halfback for the Cougars. "Oh, shit," he thought. After all of this uproar Coach Green might not even let him on the team.

He found his car and maneuvered the Ford back and forth until he got it turned out in the street, headed away from the bandstand. A frowning deputy sheriff pulled a couple of sawhorses out of the way, and Tommy was free. When he got a block from the square, he speed-shifted from second to third and left the faintest mark of rubber on the pavement. He checked the rearview mirror but figured all of the deputies were tied up downtown. He gunned the Ford straight west, letting the wind whip through the car and cool him down.

Then out to the side, just past the Magnolia station, he saw the quick wave of an arm and heard a shrill whistle, and all at once Zoette Acton was there, stepping from the curb, waving and whistling him down. Tommy hit the brakes, but skidded on by, and by the time he had shifted into reverse Zoette was at the open window on the passenger side. She bent down just a little and Tommy cut his eyes to the scooped neck of her blouse, but only for a second. He would always remember that moment.

"Can I get a ride?" she asked. "I don't live too far."

His mother would be furious if he was late, but Tommy had no choice, it was as if forever he had been headed for this one moment, the instant when Zoette Acton would step off the curb and into his life. He might never be the same again.

When Tommy didn't answer she popped open the door and slid in beside him. Zoette pointed straight ahead. "Out the Dallas highway," she said. "It's only a couple of miles." From a red leather purse she pulled a pack of Pall Malls and tapped one out. "Want one?" she asked, and Tommy shook his head. Zoette struck a kitchen match under the dash and lit up. She tossed her head back and simultaneously exhaled, a tricky move that Tommy had seen in some movie. She pulled her legs under her, as if she were sitting on a sofa.

She wore narrow strap sandals with flat heels, and her toenails flashed red and smooth. Between the sandals and her white shorts there seemed to be an endless sweep of silky brown skin. Zoette Acton had the most beautiful legs Tommy had ever seen. Her hair was a mess of black-coffee curls pulled back tight against her head and secured by a bright orange scarf.

Tommy felt dizzy, the road suddenly moving out and then back into focus as he glanced from the highway and over to Zoette. Concentrate, concentrate, he told himself. Think of something clever to say. This is your chance. "Do you like movies?" he finally asked.

Zoette exhaled again, this time through her nose, and sweet smoke wafted through the car. Tommy secretly inhaled and held his breath, knowing that the air now in his lungs was Zoette's breath. When his mother drove the car later that day she would accuse him of smoking, he figured. But he didn't care, or maybe he would drive real fast on the way back home to air it out. Or maybe he would stop at the Magnolia station and buy one of those perfumed cardboard skunks that cool guys hang from their rearview mirrors.

"Movies?" Zoette said. "What kind of movies?" She glanced at the Dairy King as they sped by, and Tommy slowed for a moment. Maybe he could buy her an ice cream cone. But that sounded too juvenile for a girl as sophisticated as Zoette. He shifted to third, gaining speed again.

"Oh, I don't know," Tommy said. "'Dead Man's Gold' is on at the Dixie . . ."

"I hate those stupid westerns," Zoette said.

"Yeah," Tommy said, his mind now quick and light. "Me, too. And I was going to say that if there had been something good on–you know, a Stewart Granger movie or something–maybe we could go."

Zoette shrugged. "Maybe," she said, but she had a look that Tommy recognized, one of boredom and impatience, a look that told him Zoette Acton yearned for things that fourteen-year-old Tommy Patterson could not dream of supplying. He sank a little and speeded up even more, ready to be alone.

At the top of a hill she pointed to the right. "Here," she said, and when Tommy pulled off the highway she flipped the stub of her Pall Mall onto the gravel driveway. Her father's furniture shop appeared to be closed, but Tommy spotted Zoette's mother out behind the trailer poking a broom handle in a black pot that was balanced over an open fire.

"Oh, crap," Zoette said. "It's wash day."

Then Tommy had an inspiration. He would make one last try, this time with something out of the ordinary, something exotic. "A helicopter's landing out at the junior college," he said. "Later on this afternoon. At four." Zoette perked up a little at that. At least Tommy thought so. "I'll be there. I've never seen a helicopter up close."

Zoette gave an indecipherable shrug and pushed the car door open. She swung her legs out. And then she swung them back in. She turned to Tommy, the first time she had looked right at him all day. “Thanks for the ride,” she said. “I wish I had a car.” Zoette looked sad and wistful and Tommy wanted to hold her, comfort her. Maybe they could just drive off together. Even for a little while more. “But my old man,” she said. “He’s always broke.”

Before Tommy could even think, or much less react, Zoette slid over next to him, her fingers on his thigh, lightly, her left breast pushed firmly into his arm, and she kissed him on the cheek. His head filled with Pall Mall smoke and a hint of strange sweetness. Her bundle of hair brushed his face when she turned away, and then she was out of the car. In a few quick strides she was gone, the trailer’s screen door banging behind her.

“Oh, Zoette! My sweet, sweet Zoette!” There were no other words, only that litany of amazement, over and over again, while Tommy pushed the Ford hard racing back into town. ❖

Chapter Seven

It wasn't all that easy for Mary Lee to maneuver the Ford across town to the Smart Shoppe, for Kate Crowder's dress shop was situated just a block-and-a-half east of the congested square. The car smelled odd, a mix of cheap perfume and . . . what? Cigarette smoke? Then she spotted a cardboard skunk hanging from the rearview mirror. Well, she thought, that explains the dreadful sweet smell. But obviously Tommy had bought it, and he didn't squander his allowance foolishly. Someone had been smoking in the car. The Holley boy, she figured. Mary Lee knew that he would come to no good. She would talk to Tommy, but not today, and certainly not tonight. But he would have to know where this sort of thing could lead.

When Mary Lee finally pulled into the black-topped parking lot in front of the little shop, her friend Kate was outside, guarding her three parking spaces from the country folks who were still pouring into town.

When Kate recognized Mary Lee and the Ford she waved her in, making a series of elaborate hand signals until the car was nosed-in just right. The Smart Shoppe was a small frame house that Kate had converted into Cottonwood's only dress shop. Some of the siding that touched the ground had rotted, and the wood shingled roof had turned gray from too many Texas summers. But Kate had painted the whole thing pink, a shocking shade of pink that for weeks had the Tuesday morning ladies' Bible class at the Central Baptist Church debating the possibility of a boycott.

A picture window took up most of the Smart Shoppe's front. From there an armless mannequin stared glassy-eyed at the street. She was decked out in a frilly red party dress that flared out just below the knee, exposing layers of petticoats. The mannequin's wig featured a daring wave that curved almost down to one eye.

Kate plopped down on the front steps and pulled one shoe off, wiping at the soft tar that coated its high heel. "These country bumpkins," she said, "coming into town with their jillion snotty-nosed young-uns, pulling their junker trucks into any open spot they can find." She rolled her eyes and slipped her shoe back on. "But not in front of my shop," she said.

Kate was "full-figured," as she liked to say, but always looked as if she had stepped straight out of a Sanger Department Store ad. She tied back her shoulder length hair with a large red bow. Kate would move about the shop, prancing and turning on the smooth pine floor, modeling the latest style for whoever might stop by. Rumor had it that Kate changed dresses three or four times a day, and saved her most provocative numbers for the traveling salesmen who parked their sample-stuffed Cadillacs out front for what some thought to be unseemly lengths of time.

"I need a dress," Mary Lee said. "I need the most perfect dress. I need shoes that match. And, and . . . " To her surprise Mary Lee felt teary. "And I need your help."

"Now, now," Kate said. "My poor Mary Lee." She pushed herself up from the steps and led her friend inside the shop, closing out the cacophony of the music and the crowd just down the street. "You, my dear, have come to the right place."

Kate, like everyone else in town, had already heard the news about Chester Carroll's confession and suicide. Sheriff Jess Sweeten had held a mid-morning news conference in front of the jail, and within an hour the sordid story had spread from store to store and house to house. After the press conference, the sheriff, a giant of a man renowned for his marksmanship and two-fisted arrests, sent a deputy north across the tracks to colored town. There he met with the Reverend William Isaacs and a couple of the church elders advising them that south of the railroad tracks would be off-limits for "colored boys" the next few days. "For your own protection," the deputy told them. "Except, of course, for employed maids, cooks and gardeners."

Right off Kate had to know how Thomas had taken the news. Mary Lee skipped the throwing up in the bathroom part and portrayed Thomas as rational and reasonable, at that very moment over at his office in a "strategy planning session."

"Excuse me for saying so," Kate said, touching Mary Lee lightly on the arm. "But wouldn't most men be mad about this, and stomp around? My Carl sure would have, bless his departed soul."

Mary Lee sighed. Kate was her dear friend, but her husband–her ex-husband Carl Crowder–hadn't "departed" in the sense that Kate's words implied. He was not dead. Not by a long shot. He was alive and well and working as a tool pusher for Delta Drilling Company over around Shreveport. "Departed" was technically correct, Mary Lee knew, but "departed soul" skewed things too much.

But that wasn't important. Everyone in town knew about Carl's departing, and no one called Kate on it. Not to her face. No, what bothered Mary Lee was that she couldn't confide to Kate how badly the morning's shocking news had upset Thomas. And her version did make Thomas appear to be lacking in feelings. But Mary Lee couldn't afford to have her husband appear weak or helpless–not with so much on the line.

So while Kate pulled dresses from the racks, and while Mary Lee tried on first this one (too frivolous), and that one (too severe), and another one (the wrong color), and still another one (better for a funeral), Mary Lee trickled out the story of Thomas' ambitions for district judge, and how the governor had crawfished out of what appeared to be his earlier commitment, and how an old stodgy like Coke Stevenson would be no help at all. "Our only hope is Congressman Johnson. It's a gamble, for sure. Even Thomas thinks the man has little chance to be senator. But he's our only hope. And he will be here tonight." She looked over at Kate, her eyes steady and determined. "I will do whatever I can to help my husband."

"Oh, hon," Kate said. "I know you will. But you need a dress to knock him out. Something that the congressman will never forget." Her face brightened, and Mary Lee could see Kate transporting herself somewhere in her imagination. "Maybe," Kate said, "if you get the chance, you can tell him you got your dress here in Cottonwood, at the Smart Shoppe."

With that Kate hurried to the back of the store and ducked through a pair of curtains. She came back in a minute dragging a long cardboard box. "The dress–your perfect dress–is in here. I know it, I know it. Fresh from the Apparel Mart in Dallas."

And the dress *was* there; Kate pulled it from the box first thing, a green satin dress with a tasteful sweetheart neckline. Its pleated peplum would accent Mary Lee's trim waist and soft shoulder pads gave the dress a feeling of substance and the latest style.

Mary Lee twirled this way and that, almost dancing as she admired the dress in the full-length mirror.

"With your hair, hon," Kate said. "The color is perfect." And it was, the glimmer of the soft green, Mary Lee's honey-colored hair, and her fair skin worked together. It was as if Kate had performed some magic spell. "Wear those pearls you have, hon, and . . . well, what can I say? You'll be a knockout."

Mary Lee nodded. She would wear her grandmother's simple string of pearls.

"Now," Kate said, "Shoes to match." She glanced down at Mary Lee's feet although she already knew her best friend wore 7-1/2's, and in no time at all found a pair of satin heels with matching flowers attached to the top of each open toe. She held them next to Mary Lee's dress.

"You are amazing," Mary Lee said.

"What do you expect?" Kate said.

Then she got serious. "Okay. You've got the perfect dress, the perfect shoes. Do your hair up fancy, and you're the belle of the ball. Now envision this. You're there. Thomas is there. And Congressman Johnson is there. What do you do?"

Mary Lee threw up her arms in frustration. "That, my dear, is the problem." Then a knowing smile moved across her face and she nodded. "A problem that I may be able to solve. If only I dare."

"You have to tell me," Kate said. "I love, love, love things that are daring. It's so boring around here."

So Mary Lee told Kate about the song that kept overtaking her at the most inappropriate moments, the images that came to her mind while she sang along to "The Gypsy." "I even dance–all alone. 'Stop that Mary Lee,' I tell myself. 'You're not a girl.' But it all seems to be out of my control."

"Oh, I love it, Mary Lee. You're the only friend I have who would admit to such a thing." Kate leaned close. "A secret now. Just between the two of us."

Mary Lee nodded.

"Sometimes, after I close the shop I turn off all the lights. And–oh, this is so embarrassing. You're sure you won't tell!"

"I'd never tell," she said. "You can trust me."

"Well, I find a negligee, something black and red from the bottom drawer there. And I dance, too. Not to 'The Gypsy,' but to whatever I can pick up on the radio. Mostly out of Shreveport. And you know what?"

Mary Lee's eyes opened wide in anticipation.

Kate's voice dropped to a whisper. "All the while I'm dancing, I dream–oh, I'm ashamed to say this–that a certain

Dallas accessories salesman, who will go unnamed, but who drives a new baby blue Cadillac, will stop by the shop." Kate swallowed and took a deep breath. "And that he will sneak in with a bottle of champagne behind his back. And we will sip champagne, and I won't have to dance alone. And . . . well, that's enough," she laughed. "Probably more than enough. But, Mary Lee, we got completely off the track. Back to your business. How will you know what in the world to do tonight?"

"I," Mary Lee bravely said, "am going to see a gypsy."

"A gypsy?" Kate asked. "Here in Cottonwood?"

"Out on the Dallas highway. 'Card and palm readings.' That's what the sign says. Or what it used to say before the Baptists stole it. She's a gypsy as far as I can tell. Can't you see? That song that's been haunting me, the one that won't leave me alone, is trying to tell me something, give me direction. And now I'm going to listen."

"Oh, my God, "Kate said. "Do you dare? Do you really dare? Oh, hon, I will be at the reception tonight. You can tell me everything. I've never met a real live congressman, and I've got to see you in action. Oh, I just can't wait." ❖

Chapter Eight

Outside the Smart Shoppe the clatter and screeching from the courthouse square overwhelmed Mary Lee and, despite the heat of the afternoon, she rolled the car windows tight before she pulled away. Still, she could feel the thump, thump, thump of an amplified bass resonating through the car, pounding in her head. She found herself vacillating about her plan. What had seemed so clear, so certain a course of action earlier in the day–and even certain just moments before she stepped out of Kate's dress shop–now seemed foolish and silly. A gypsy. For crying out loud! What in the world would Thomas say? Hocus-pocus, for sure.

So she turned the car east, away from the courthouse square, away from the intolerable noise and confusion and chaos. Perhaps a drive, leaving that clamor and the conflict of her life behind, would help clear her head. She needed to be at her best by tonight. Thomas would need her.

She drove east, out the Tyler highway, determined to find a country road where the peace and quiet might be restorative. The houses out this highway were Cottonwood's finest: a two-story, red brick Georgian with white columns; a New Orleans style bungalow with the curve of a wraparound front porch, screened in to deter flies and mosquitoes. The president of the Farmers and Merchants Bank and his wife lived there. Their lives seemed as smooth and well-maintained as the sweep of carpet grass out front.

A Negro gardener made his way slowly up the front walk, kneeling now and then along that brick path to clip a stray weed or pick up a yellow, curved magnolia leaf, intent on eliminating even the tiniest hindrances to the owners' harmony and order.

Mary Lee knew her life would never have harmony and order, even if Thomas did overcome this dreadful difficulty and become a state district judge. Money wouldn't fix the disorder of Mary Lee's life, nor would Thomas's success and prestige.

When Mary Lee reached the edge of town she rolled the windows back down and let the warm air whip through the Ford, and in a few minutes she felt her tension start to slide away.

Three highways intersected at Cottonwood, the two east/west roads crossed in a Y, like opened scissors at the west end of town, diverging to either Corsicana or to Dallas. Heading east, these two highways split at the courthouse square and the only one of import–unless you were a tomato packer picking up a fresh load from a truck farm–was Highway 31. It hit the east Texas piney woods in twenty or so miles, and then led on in to Tyler.

The roads north and south were of little consequence. Highway 19 north would take you across stretches of sand hills and post oak flats to Canton where on the first Monday of each month those so inclined could trade for a good 'coon hound or cow dog or double barrel shotgun.

Heading south, Highway 19 led into sparsely settled sand fields and pastures, the only landmark worth one whit of notice a concrete block café where the country club set of Cottonwood gathered, tipsy, late on Saturday nights for sixteen ounce t-bones and hand-cut french fries and quarter heads of lettuce smothered with orange dressing. More important the proprietor would bring to their tables set-ups for the brown bagged bottles of Wild Turkey–illegal in this dry county.

Mary Lee drove east, and if she had the time might have kept on going straight to Tyler where there was a more than decent department store downtown and a couple of stylish dress shops on a boulevard south of the town's square.

In a few minutes she spotted a farm to market road that led off to the north; a faded sign tacked on a cedar fence post read, "Sand Flats 5 miles." Without thinking, as if someone else controlled the wheel of the car, and her fate, Mary Lee turned the car off the highway, and then she hesitated a moment, eyeing the sandy, rutted road.

She wouldn't want to sink the car's wheels into this east Texas blow sand, for the sand was as fine as wheat flour and by mid-summer more treacherous than winter's mud could ever be. But this early in the year, with the rains that they had been lucky enough to have, she figured the road would be no problem. And sure enough, the Ford found the ruts and moved effortlessly along.

It was not yet three. Mary Lee had plenty of time. Her new dress and shoes sparkly and shiny in the back seat, and honestly, she wanted to avoid Thomas for as long as possible. He would be either stewing and muttering to himself, or depressingly silent. No, she would stay away as long as she dared.

Mary Lee passed fields of blossoming tomato plants and sprawling watermelon vines. Bull nettles and goat weeds dotted the middles of sandy rows. Here and there rusted three-wire fences surrounded pastures of bony cows, and sometimes, set back from the road, Mary Lee caught a gray glimpse of a sagging house, or a man following a harnessed mule down crooked rows.

She watched for mailboxes and read the names: Cummings and Jenkins and Slagle and Racker, names that sounded familiar, some of the children who lived along this road Tommy's classmates over the years. And she felt herself sink, realizing that the boys who lived in these dismal houses with their tilted, stinking outhouses and their hand dug wells and blank-eyed parents were perhaps Tommy's school friends.

And, God forbid, Tommy might be attracted to one of those girls whose free and easy ways might be impossible for

Tommy to ignore. And he might even have to marry one of them and . . . oh, she couldn't bear to think about it.

When she got home she would tell Thomas–she would insist–that they move back to Dallas. She would learn to control her tongue and even her thoughts around Adelle. She would be as nicey-nice as necessary. She would do anything to save Tommy from this trap he might innocently fall into.

But Mary Lee knew she couldn't ever be nicey-nice–not to her mother-in-law–and *she* felt trapped, trapped by all of the foolish mistakes and decisions of her life. If she had only stayed in college and completed her teacher's certificate, she could have been teaching in a nice high school somewhere, maybe back in Tyler–no, she wouldn't want to be that close to her parents. But maybe Waco or Fort Worth. There were good schools there.

And maybe she would have met some decent sort of history teacher who smoked a pipe and had a big dog that sat at his feet while he read–or maybe even wrote–some history of a war somewhere exotic. A man of passion, who knew when to push back from his desk and ask–no tell–Mary Lee to follow him to the bedroom.

But in Tyler there had been that young farm and ranch real estate man in the office where she worked the year after she left the teachers' college, the year that Thomas finished law school. Oh, what was his name? His name had faded away, but she could remember his face and his thighs and his brown, muscular arms. He had a quick wink, Mary Lee remembered that, and wore his hat at a rakish angle. Even then, with the depression dragging down the entire country, he drove a new Pontiac. A young man from Kilgore, and his family owned enough of that East Texas oil field not to let a little old depression bother them. At the time Mary Lee thought that he might have his eye on her. But oh no, she was too loyal to Thomas to even think such a thing. So sad.

Suddenly, just as she was determined to put that Tyler real estate man out of her mind, his name came to her from out of nowhere. Horace Ledbetter. And she remembered the Pontiac now, a coupe, with a rumble seat, and she could see plain as anything the Chief Pontiac radiator cap, with the Indian's feathers and braids swept back as if from the wind.

Oh. She had seen Chief Pontiac from inside the car, she now was certain, for she could remember the way that lights–a string of yellow lights–dangled over a dance pavilion and glistened on the chrome. Yes, out at Tyler State Park. And there were couples dancing on the open pavilion. And there was a band. And again, out of nowhere, Mary Lee heard the music from that night, indeed, the specific song, that played as she sat next to Horace Ledbetter and stared out at the lights, and she could almost hear Bing Crosby crooning on about finding his million dollar baby in a five and ten cent store. What had happened next she couldn't remember. Maybe she hadn't been quite so loyal to Thomas as she had thought. But Mary Lee was only twenty at the time, and lonely. It was an insignificant flirtation. Harmless.

And now, seventeen years later the possibility–the remote possibility–of another, even less significant flirtation. This time with Byron Bostick–and even that might be only in her imagination–to keep her spirits up. So, so sad. She sighed and felt her eyes well up, but they seemed to fill not from the sadness, but from some anger she couldn't quite bring into focus. She shook her head. "Get a hold of yourself, Mary Lee," she said, and tried to concentrate on the narrow, sandy ruts.

In places the road narrowed and dipped, and once the car rattled across a plank bridge that hid a trickle of murky water. In those creek bottoms the woods stood dark and thick with hickory and pecan trees, and on the hillsides, interspersed with the fields, she passed dense and shadowed stands of post oak and sumac.

Suddenly she realized that it was in one of these very thickets that Chester Carroll had overpowered the struggling Corrine Abernathy, and Mary Lee tried to envision the attack–the loneliness of the road, the awful silence that hung all around, except for Chester's hard driving breaths, and Corrine's thrashing and screams. Oh my God, Mary Lee thought, and it did happen right around here, for she calculated that Sand Flat and Jensen's Store must be just down the road.

An unusually dark and dense stand of scrub oak edged out almost to the road ahead of her, the tree limbs pushing through the barbed wire fence, extending so near to the road that Mary Lee slowed the car and eased to the left, but felt the sand grab her wheels and she came to a stop.

At that moment, when she stared into the shadows of the trees, Mary Lee had an impulse–no, it was stronger than that–she felt an urge from somewhere primeval to leave the car in the road and abandon herself to those dense woods. She would stretch out on a bed of oak leaves and let the sun flicker its way across the pattern of her dress. She would experience the excitement of vulnerability, of the possibility of something forbidden. But all in the safety of her isolation, of being hidden.

But the woods held hordes of seed ticks, and chiggers infested the weed-ridden bar ditch Mary Lee would have to wade through to get to the woods. Her dress would need to be washed, and how would she explain the dirt and grass stains to Elberta when she came to do the household chores on Thursday? So many decisions to make and none of them felt right.

She should be home right now, helping Tommy, pressing out his good slacks, making sure the hem didn't need to be let down. That boy grows like the sucker on a wild rose, she thought. He might even need a snack to tide him over until tonight. A good mother would have some oatmeal cookies baked, and she glanced down the road halfheartedly looking for a gap in the tree line where she might turn the Ford around. Mary Lee eased the car back into the ruts and pulled ahead, the car scraping past a single limb that reached into the road.

Another mailbox ahead, a dirt road for a turnaround there, but as she slowed she spotted the name on the mailbox, Edd Abernathy, painted black in careless freehand on a dented mailbox. From the road Mary Lee tried to spot the house, but couldn't. She gunned the Ford, anyway. For certain she did not want to come across Mr. Abernathy. She checked the rearview mirror and, in a panic, locked both car doors. Her hands trembled uncontrollably, and she gripped the steering wheel tight in an effort to stay on the road.

But maybe she *should* "just happen" to run into Mr. Abernathy. If he was a reasonable man he would accept Mary Lee's explanation of what happened. How Thomas' name was literally drawn out of a hat, that her husband didn't want the thankless job of defending Chester Carroll at all, but that he was a man of honor and felt it was his patriotic and civic duty–as much a duty as serving in the armed forces–to carry out the mandates of the judicial system.

Perhaps she could persuade Mr. Abernathy to make some conciliatory statement that would appear in the *Tyler Telegraph* for all the world to see, and Thomas would be back in good graces with the governor, and he would indeed be the next district judge. Then they could move–to Palestine or Jacksonville, perhaps–and start a new life with new friends, and maybe they could afford to send Tommy to a private school in Dallas, and Mary Lee could . . . could . . . and there her dream faltered. Well, she could be a good wife . . . at least try to be a better wife to Thomas. Yes, that would be enough. It might have to be enough. She sighed.

In a couple of minutes Mary Lee guided the Ford around a curve, slowing as the wheels momentarily lost the ruts, and suddenly, just ahead, she saw Jensen's Store. Mary Lee stopped at the crossroads, and with the Ford's engine roughly idling, she eyed the place. The store was a faded gray rectangle of a building with a corrugated tin roof. A single Gulf gas pump with a glass globe on top stood out front next to a green metal box with a hand pump that held kerosene. A lanky yellow dog lay in the shade of the front porch and raised its head to snap at a fly. Behind the store was a backstop constructed of chicken wire and a couple of benches that bordered what appeared to be a baseball field.

Mary Lee might just stop at the store, for she certainly could use a cold strawberry soda, and maybe a small sliver of ice would be floating in the cooler box. She would wrap it in a tissue, and back in the car wipe its coolness across her forehead. Yes, that sounded like a good plan.

She parked the car out to one side and made her way across a scattering of rusted soda pop tops that served as the parking lot's surface. Three wooden steps led up to the plank porch where the dog thumped its tail twice at Mary Lee, then lifted its leg and licked his thin, pink penis. Mary Lee quickly looked away and stepped inside the store, easing the screen door shut behind her.

A big-headed man with sloped shoulders and thinning red hair looked up from behind the counter, but showed no surprise at the sight of this strange woman entering his store.

"Kin I he'p you?" he finally asked, and Mary Lee pointed to the cooler box in the front of the room. "Oh, something cold to drink," she said. Sodas of all kinds and colors leaned this way and that among the chunks of ice, and Mary Lee dug around root beers and cream sodas and Chocolate Soldiers and Dr Peppers until she found a Nehi strawberry soda and pulled it up, letting it drip back in the box for a moment before she popped off the cap with an opener that hung from a string.

The man–she figured it was Mr. Jensen–stared at her for

minute, and then went back to sorting a stack of nails, tossing them into various tin buckets.

A single bare light bulb hung from a rafter, dangling little more than head-high from a twisted cord. A black wood-burning stove sat in the center of the store, surrounded by a couple of cane-bottomed, slat-back chairs and a low wooden bench. As her eyes adjusted to the dim light, Mary Lee spotted an old man in the shadows at the back of the store. He sat leaned forward in a chair, balancing himself with both hands that gripped the top of a wooden cane. A spittoon rested on the floor between his feet. He didn't look up.

A glass cake cover on the counter protected a hunk of rat trap cheese, and the walls were lined with cans of red beans and Vienna sausage and sardines.

"A nickel," Mr. Jensen said. "For the soda, it's a nickel. If you drink it here. The bottle's another penny if you take it with you."

"Oh," Mary Lee said, "I'll just drink it here." She sat the drink on the counter and dug around in her purse for a nickel. She found a dime and slid it across the counter, then picked up a package of cheese crackers from a box and held it up.

Mr. Jensen nodded. "Even Steven," he said, and rang up the dime.

Even Steven, Mary Lee thought. He's not the most original fellow in the world. It was a good thing she hadn't pulled a ten dollar bill out–he would have had to send out for arithmetic help. Mary Lee had usually found these country store owners to be fairly intelligent–often a little brighter and more knowledgeable than their neighbors, blank-faced men who seemed to have trouble getting from one end of a row of crowder peas to the other.

But if Mr. Jensen is the best this community could do, she might want to re-think her plan to confront Edd Abernathy.

Mary Lee moved around the store, past shelves of tools and screws and work gloves. She dawdled at a table that held stacked boxes of Remington shotgun shells and long rifle .22s. All the while Mary Lee rehearsed what she would say, how she would ask Mr. Jensen where Edd Abernathy was, if he might be at his house or working his field. But she needed some reason for this. And still, she wasn't sure it was the best thing to do. She knew what Thomas would say. He would blow his top, for sure–unless she was able to come to a truce with Mr. Abernathy. If that happened, then what could he say! Mary Lee finished the cheese crackers and strawberry soda, and slid the bottle into a divided, tilted box. That's probably lunch, she thought. She fished around in the cooler until she found a small piece of ice. She held it up. "Do you mind?" she asked. Mr. Jensen shrugged, and Mary Lee wrapped it in a tissue just as she had planned.

"I don't suppose you know where I could find Mr. Edd Abernathy, do you?" Mary Lee hesitated. She felt her heart flutter, and knew her face was flushed. She casually wiped the cool tissue across her forehead.

"Well," Jensen said. "His place is back down the road a piece. Towards 31. You try him at the house?"

"Well, yes," Mary Lee said. "I mean no, I didn't do that. But yes, I suppose I could," Mary Lee stammered. "I just thought he might stop by here, and I am in a little bit of a hurry to get back to town."

"He ain't at the house," Jensen said. "Stopped by early. A while back. Pumped five gallons in that truck of his. There was Abernathys ever'where. Four in the cab and a half-dozen in the back. That old truck sure was packed. All of 'em as far as I could tell. But for that middle girl. Corrine." He stopped then, and waited, but Mary Lee didn't even blink. "She don't go to town no more. Yeah, I reckon the bunch of 'em made it in to Cottonwood, for the fiddlin'. If their tires didn't blow."

"Oh," Mary Lee sighed, "I should have thought of that. The Fiddlers' Contest." Thank God, she thought, I've wiggled out of this one. What in the world am I doing anyway? What in the world would I have said to Edd Abernathy?

"Abernathy's old lady signed for the gas and a dime's worth of cheese. Said she had a ton of 'tater salad and had crispyed up a couple of fryers." Then Jensen leaned forward, his hands flat on the counter. "Old Edd, he picked up a box of .410 shells. Bird shot. Won't be bird season 'til fall, I told him. But he just laughed. That man don't know the proper time for things. Or the proper ways, neither."

".410 shells?" Mary Lee asked. "You mean for a shotgun?"

"Lots of folks in town, Mrs. Patterson?" he asked. "Lawyer Patterson in town?"

Mary Lee now flushed for certain. "Do I know you?" she asked, in as uppity a voice as she could muster. "Why do you think that I am Mrs. Patterson?"

Jensen grinned.

Mary Lee nodded and backed towards the screen door, then turned and half-stumbled onto the porch and down the rickety steps and hurried to her car.

The road back to Highway 31 seemed longer than before, even though she pushed the Ford all she dared. Mary Lee's first reaction was panic, intertwined with terror. Edd Abernathy would shoot Thomas to avenge his daughter, and it was up to Mary Lee to warn her husband–if she could only get there before it was too late. But by the time she had bounced across the creek and climbed the last long hill out to the hard-top highway her panic and terror had turned into a feeling of foolishness.

Would Mr. Jensen have grinned when he told her about Abernathy buying the bird shot if he thought his neighbor might really shoot Thomas? Mary Lee strongly suspected that Jensen fabricated his vague and laconic statements as part of a game, some sort of revenge that country folk inflicted upon gullible ladies from town. Well, his stupid country fabrications won't work on me, Mary Lee swore as she turned onto the highway and headed back towards Cottonwood. She had a mind to go back and tell Jensen off, to let him know that Mary Lee Patterson was nobody's fool. But she still had more important problems to deal with. She would forget about Jensen and concentrate on the reception for Congressman Johnson.

But Kate's words came back to her: "Now envision this. You're there. Thomas is there. And Congressman Johnson is there. What do you do?" Mary Lee remembered her answer. "A problem that I may be able to solve. If only I dare." She hurried back towards Cottonwood, all the while repeating over and over, "If only I dare, if only I dare, if only I dare." She skirted the town square, circling through familiar neighborhoods, then finally moving past a lumber yard that faced the Dallas highway. There she turned west, away from Cottonwood, still repeating, "If I only dare, if I only dare," to give her courage.

A couple of miles out of town Mary Lee slowed, then pulled off the ragged edge of the highway onto the gravel shoulder. Up ahead she could see the old candy factory, now with a rough-painted sign out front that simply said FURNITURE FOR SALE. Mary Lee pulled forward a little and she spotted the green trailer out back. A gray 2 X 4 propped open the trailer's only door, and all three windows across the side were rolled out. Mary Lee moved her lips as she read a new poster board sign taped to the side of the trailer. "CARD AND PALM READINGS." She felt her heart flutter again, and she sank down in the seat a little and looked away when a car came over the hill towards her. When all was clear she gunned the Ford forward and pulled in the driveway. She parked out to the side, easing the car into the shade cast by a sycamore tree, a good distance from the trailer.

Almost hidden behind the trailer, out past a wisp of smoke that rose from a rusted trash barrel, a girl was pinning a basket of wet clothes to a sagging line. She appeared to be fifteen or so, her skin almost bronze, and her dark mass of hair swayed and bounced as she bent and stretched with the clothes.

For a moment Mary Lee thought the girl might be a Mexican, but then she remembered that she had seen the furniture man at Spencer's Hardware and he had appeared to be Italian or Greek–definitely not Mexican. This had to be his daughter.

Mary Lee waited while the girl finished her chore. A healthy enough fifteen-year old, Mary Lee thought, watching her bend gracefully for the damp clothes, then shake them out.

When finally she turned, swinging the empty basket by one handle, the girl noticed the Ford, and gave Mary Lee a big wave. She dropped the basket and ran towards the car, stopping, looking surprised when Mary Lee stuck her head out the window and tentatively waved back.

In a moment the girl turned and raced back to the trailer, slamming the screen door behind her. Now what was that all about, Mary Lee wondered. She obviously thought I was someone else. She shook her head. Teenagers can be so awkward, so easily embarrassed.

A couple of cars zoomed down the road, heading into Cottonwood. Mary Lee could hear them before they topped the hill, so she waited for a long stretch of quiet, and then hurried from the shade of the tree to the steps of the trailer. She eased inside the screen door and closed it behind her so that she felt less visible from the highway.

The interior of the trailer was dim, but in a moment Mary Lee made out the figure of a woman. She sat at the only table in the room, surrounded by a half-dozen beaded, stuffed pillows.

The woman didn't look up, but shuffled a deck of cards, then fanned them out on the slick-topped table. "I've been expecting you," she said. Mary Lee moved a couple of steps towards her. The woman looked familiar. She had long, black eyelashes and bold red lips and a scarf wrapped expertly around her head. The sleeves of her sequined blouse billowed out, and silver bracelets jangled when she shuffled the cards. Silver rings adorned her fingers and circles of hammered silver hung from her ears.

The woman on the record cover, Mary Lee thought. She looks just like the fortune teller on the cover of "The Gypsy," and silently the melody swam through her head.

"Come," the woman said. "I am Madame Acton. For you I will read the tea leaves." She reached for a tea pot on the counter and removed the lid. With a silver spoon she stirred the tea slowly. Then quickly, before the tea leaves could settle, she filled a white porcelain cup.

"And then I will read your palm. Or perhaps the cards would be better. We will wait and see what the tea leaves tell us." She motioned for Mary Lee to sit across from her.

"Well, yes," Mary Lee said, slipping onto the so-thick cushion of the chair. "That sounds fine, but I really need some advice. You see this is a very important day and my husband . . ." Madame Acton shook her head and held up her hand. "There is nothing you can tell me. Nothing that you can ask me. Your fate, your future, is already determined. There is nothing you can do to change it. All I can do is reveal it." Mary Lee gasped. The trailer was too warm, the air heavy with the smell of fried onions. She looked around for one of the open windows, but all of the curtains were tightly drawn across them.

"If you don't want to know the future, then you may still leave." Madame Acton leaned back against the pillows and gestured towards the door.

"Well, I guess I can stay. But how much will it cost? I mean for all three readings?"

"It is nothing," Madame Acton said with a frown, as if Mary Lee had insulted her. "What is it worth for you to know your future?" She peered into the cup where the tea leaves had settled. "Five dollars is all."

"Oh, my goodness," Mary Lee said, but she dug through her purse and in a moment counted out five ones on the table. Madame Acton smiled. "Let us begin." The beaded curtains towards the back of the trailer parted then and the girl slipped through. "Ah, Zoette," Madame Acton said. Then she turned to Mary Lee. "My daughter Zoette, Mrs. Patterson."

"How did you know . . . ?" Mary Lee sputtered. "Now I had rather this, this meeting to be just between the two of us. You know the people in town." Madame Acton ignored her. She turned to Zoette, a question on her face.

"To town," Zoette replied to her mother's unasked question. "Just for a little while." "Not after dark," Madame Acton said, and then with a flick of her hand shooed Zoette out the door.

"Now," she said, nodding at Mary Lee. "Come closer. Let us begin. Place your hand over the cup. Like this." Madame Acton held her hand above the cup, careful not to touch it.

Mary Lee wiggled forward in her chair and held her hand out, giving it a little wag.

"On the cup," Madame Acton said, her voice impatient. "But lightly."

Mary Lee did as she was told, lowering her hand gently onto the porcelain cup. The steam from the tea warmed a circle on the palm of her hand.

"You must keep your hand there, without moving, for two minutes. The energy," she said, "will be transferred to the tea leaves." Madame Acton pulled a gauzy curtain across the open window, then settled back against a satin pillow and closed her eyes.

A red wasp buzzed against the curtain and one car slowed, then sped on by. Mary Lee wished she had parked out back.

What if someone from town recognized her car parked there under the tree and stopped? Maybe someone well-intentioned, stopping to help her, for gypsies were notorious for kidnapping women and children. How would she ever explain that to Thomas?

"Enough," Madame Acton finally said. She lifted Mary Lee's hand and took the cup, nodding with approval. She swirled the cup, holding it over a chipped blue bowl, tilting it, sloshing the tea so that in a few moments the cup was empty. Madame Acton held it up, turning it so Mary Lee could see the pattern of leaves stuck to the inside.

"The leaves have found their pattern. Each one is absolutely unique, you know." Madame Acton scrutinized the interior of the cup once more, turning it this way and that, holding it up to the light of the window. She tilted her head to one side and ran her tongue across her lips until they glistened. "This pattern," she said, "is most unusual." She gazed across at Mary Lee. Her eyes glazed over and her voice lowered to not much more than a whisper and the words no longer seemed to be hers. "A bottle," she said, and pointed a scarlet fingernail to what Mary Lee saw as only a clump of soggy leaves. "And here is a moon." Madame Acton turned the cup once more, studying it intently. "Now this appears to be half a heart shape, and this," she said with a nod, "an unlit candle." Madame Acton leaned back, her skin now glistening, her eyes closed once again. "A bottle, a moon, and half a heart. Temptation, change, and someone to show you the way."

Mary Lee's heart fluttered and she felt as if she might faint, but she leaned forward and peered cautiously into the cup where Madame Acton slowly divined her fate. ❖

Chapter Nine

The local junior college had opened the year before, starting off with a couple of buildings and an expanse of vacant field that were part of the abandoned county fairgrounds. That undeveloped field–a half mile from downtown Cottonwood–turned out to be the only sizeable place near town where a helicopter could safely land. Robert Newsome, the county Democratic chairman who would be Congressman Johnson's official host, had been advised to find a place without electric wires or tall trees for the helicopter, but it had to be near the square, so that the folks at the Fiddlers' Contest would break away from the festivities down there to greet the candidate for senator.

The new college campus was a dozen blocks from the Patterson house–an easy bike ride for Tommy if his mother didn't show up before four. If she had gone to Kate Crowder's for a new dress, he knew there was no way his mother would be back in time.

Thomas Patterson would not be a part of the welcoming party, but he and Mary Lee would wait and make their strategic move for the congressman's support after six, when the barbecue reception would begin out at the country club.

When Tommy had pulled up in front of the house earlier in the afternoon, his mother had dashed out onto the front porch. "Just leave it running, honey," she yelled, and hurried back in to grab her purse. By the time Tommy had made certain the car was in neutral and yanked on the emergency brake, his mother was there to take his place behind the wheel.

"Is what they're saying in town true?" Tommy asked, one hand on the door as if he could hold the car there until he got an answer. "I mean about Daddy and that Chester Carroll."

"As bad as they all say and worse," Mary Lee said. She rolled her eyes. "Tell your daddy that I'm at Kate's. I'll be home later, after I find the perfect dress. Oh, and remember, we're all going to the barbecue at six. We–your father and I–are going to need you." She patted his hand and with a roar and a grinding of gears she had taken off, blowing Tommy an air kiss out the window.

At three-thirty Tommy pumped up a low tire on his Schwinn and pedaled off from the house. It was too early, he knew, because the junior college was less than ten minutes away, but if Zoette should be there, Tommy didn't want her to see him pulling up on a bicycle.

He still wore his jeans and sneakers, but had dug around in the bottom drawer of a chest until he found a sky-blue short-sleeved shirt, one that Elberta had starched and ironed and folded. "A Sunday shirt," Gene would have called it, but for Tommy it was part of his strategy to impress Zoette.

At the field next to the junior college several men were stringing a rope around some wooden poles to mark off the landing area for the helicopter. They pulled it taut and then tied red mechanics' rags on the rope every few feet. While they worked they kept glancing at the sky, as if they worried that the helicopter might descend upon them before the landing site was ready.

So far only a couple dozen people had shown up, mostly boys, and several men with the sleeves of their white dress shirts rolled twice. Every now and then one of them lifted his straw hat to shade his eyes as he squinted into the sun. Then he would shake his head and fan himself with the hat for a minute before carefully angling it back on his head.

Off to one side the men had erected a war surplus canopy, and underneath the overhang Tommy spotted a cooler of iced-down sodas and moved slowly that way. There in the shade, a couple of men in short-brimmed dress hats and white shirts and ties stood talking. They had folded their suit coats over the backs of two folding chairs. Robert Newsome, the county attorney, Tommy recognized from hanging around the courthouse when his father had tried a case over Easter vacation. Newsome had a reputation as an opinionated, argumentative lawyer, but he was old now, the skin on his face transparent enough to expose the pattern of his bones. Tufts of white hair curled up around his hat. His voice was wispy, but still had some fire behind it. "No way on God's green earth will the man show up," he was saying when Tommy drew near. "Not now and not tonight." He lit a cigarette with a silver lighter, then popped the lid shut and slid it into his pocket.

"Now Robert," the other man said. He was a man of substantial girth, who wheezed when he talked. "Don't sell Patterson short. He may have his tail tucked between his legs today, but he's a shrewd one. I wouldn't put it past him to try and take center stage yet. He's salivating over that judgeship. Everybody knows that."

"Salivating won't do any good," Newsome said. "If nobody tosses him a bone." The big man gave a wheezing laugh.

The men who had been stringing the rope for the landing area and tying on the flags made their way under the canopy. One of them, red-faced and rawboned, whipped out his handkerchief and mopped his forehead. "Hot as a nigger on election day," he said, and the fellows with him grinned in agreement.

"Help yourself to a soft drink, Grady," Newsome said. "Cool down a little." Newsome cleared his throat and spit out to one side. He wiped his shirt sleeve across his mouth, and gave it a quick inspection. “But I’d not nigger this or nigger that when Congressman Johnson lands. That big old boy might just whack you upside the head.”

Grady snorted. “Huh. Him and what damned army? Don’t tell me that Johnson fellow’s another nigger lover. Well, shit fire, we already got one in the county–that damned lawyer Patterson–and he’s one too many for me.” He popped the cap off an RC Cola and stared all around, as if he was daring someone to challenge him. “Patterson’s a goddamned chicken-shit.”

Tommy stepped from where he waited at the corner of the canopy and into the shade. He was trembling, and his lips were so dry he could hardly speak. But finally, his voice came out hoarse and strained. “You can’t call my daddy a chicken-shit,” he said. “He’s not a chicken-shit at all.” Tommy was afraid he would cry, but he knew that would ruin everything.

“Well, well,” Grady said. “This must be the son of a chicken-shit,” and he gave a high-pitched laugh. “That’s a good one, huh boys? Maybe you and your daddy liked it when Chester Carroll was out and free, when he was still around looking for some other white girl to attack. Maybe you wouldn’t mind if he had de-filed your mama the way he did my cousin Corrine. No,” he said, and spit out the side, “I reckon that would be a little different.”

Tommy wanted to charge Grady, and he figured if he hit him low with his shoulder he might knock him down. But he would be no match for a grown man, not one as strong as Grady. Tommy clenched and unclenched his fists, waiting, determined not to back down.

“Now Grady,” Newsome said, stepping between him and Tommy. “I don’t blame you for being upset, but all that chicken-shit stuff is a little out of line. All things find their own level, if you only let them be. And Patterson, he’ll pay a price for this.

Already has." He took a drag from his cigarette and then pointed it at Tommy. "He's just a kid."

"Goddamn baby," Grady said, and with that Tommy charged. He hit the big man in the groin with his shoulder and Grady crumpled with a grunt, dragging Tommy down with him. But he was quick and stout and in a flash he had rolled on top of Tommy, pinning his arms down with his knees.

"Now you know how Corrine might have felt, boy, with that nigger astride her." He began to rhythmically slap Tommy's face, alternating his open hands.

Grady stopped then for a minute, breathing hard, and Tommy struggled to move, but he couldn't. He turned his head to the side as drops of Grady's sweat splattered across his face. Grady reached for the buttons on the fly of his overalls and began methodically to unbutton them. "Now this is how that colored boy did it to Corrine." He grinned up at Newsome, gave him a quick wink. "If I can just get my big old red-headed pecker unwound I'll show you what rapin's all about. You might just whistle a different tune then. You and your chicken-shit daddy, too."

"Hey, Grady," Newsome said, tossing his cigarette to one side. "That's enough now, you hear?"

"Man, oh man," someone outside the canopy hollered. "There it comes. Johnson's helicopter." And with the whomp, whomp, whomp of its blades, the helicopter made its first pass over the field, which by now was thick with mostly country folks.

Grady pushed himself up, breathing hard. He stood over Tommy and wiped one sleeve across his face. He pointed at the boy, who struggled to his knees. "You want some more? I can finish with you later. I've got more where that come from. You understand?" He brushed off his pants and found his RC Cola. He threw his shoulders back and chugged the drink, then stomped outside and moved off into the crowd.

"The sins of the fathers," Newsome muttered under his breath. "You all right, son?"

Tommy pulled up the tail of his shirt and wiped at his eyes and nose. His cheeks felt blistered. He nodded to Newsome and struggled to his feet. He reached in the cooler for some ice water and sloshed it on his face, and without a word he stepped out into the glare.

The helicopter circled out past a line of trees, then tilted to one side as it headed back.

A hand clapped Tommy on his shoulder, and he jumped, afraid in that instant that Grady had come back to finish the whipping. But it was his buddy Gene, not even looking at Tommy at all, but shading his eyes to watch the helicopter return from the west. "Man, did you see that?" Gene asked. "I told you we should have built that gyro-copter." Then he glanced at Tommy. "Where were you? Where you been?" Then he moved back a step. "Man, what got a hold of you?"

"Do I look that bad?" Tommy asked, and Gene rolled his eyes. "Not good, for sure," he said.

But then the helicopter slowed as it whipped its way over the crowd. It seemed to fill the sky above them like a giant black dragonfly. LYNDON JOHNSON U.S. SENATE stood out in bold white letters across both sides. Tommy spotted three men inside, but the helicopter was big enough to hold more. A trumpet-shaped speaker stuck out from the front, and in a moment a voice boomed out over the field. "This is Lyndon Johnson, the next United States senator from the great state of Texas."

The helicopter circled over the crowd once more, but this time hovered a little too low, and the whip of its blades sucked up a funnel of sand and grassburrs. Straw hats flew in all directions, and women grabbed at skirts that threatened to end up over their heads. Folks were coughing and wheezing; they turned their backs to the helicopter and in a panic scrambled out of the way.

The canopy next to the two boys lifted, billowing like an army-green balloon and then collapsed, taking down Robert Newsome. The county attorney's companion was too stout to topple, and he stood, thrashing around, trapped under the sagging canvas.

From the speaker on the nose of the helicopter Tommy heard a deep voice. "Take it up, goddamn it! Take the son of a bitch up!" And suddenly the helicopter rose and eased to one side and took off for the grove of woods again.

Gene flopped to the ground, laughing so hard that at first Tommy thought he had got hurt and was crying.

By the time the helicopter circled back around a bunch of cars had sputtered to life, racing away with a good number of the crowd. The helicopter finally settled down in the roped-off area, and in a moment a man hopped out of the cabin and ducking under the still rotating blades, tethered the wheels to a couple of stakes.

Tommy now could see Lyndon Johnson through the helicopter's glass bubble. He grinned and raised his hand in a salute of greeting to the folks crowding around, but all the while Tommy could tell he was telling the pilot off, but good. Then Johnson's front man emerged and waited on the helicopter's step while the blades whined down to a stop. Then the aide began to speak in an animated way as if he were the ringmaster in a circus and he had a cage of big cats behind him that would soon be released. He went on detailing the rigors of Johnson's campaign–how many miles and how many stops and how big the crowds. He took a deep breath then, looking around, finally realizing that there were only fifty or sixty people still there, maybe only half of them voting age.

"And here we are in . . ." and he glanced down at a 3 X 5 card that he carried, "in Cottonwood, Texas, the home of blackeyed peas and watermelons, the home of the world famous Old Fiddlers' Contest."

Suddenly Lyndon Johnson emerged from the cabin and with the nudge of an elbow moved his spokesman aside. He waved his Stetson and nodded to the sprinkling of applause. He looked elegant in a sharkskin suit and a wide, colorful tie. He was bigger than Tommy had imagined–taller, especially standing on the step of the helicopter. His hair was slicked straight back, but still a little curly on the sides, and his hands and his ears seemed huge.

A photographer from the local paper moved in close with his camera, snapping shots of the helicopter. From inside the pilot waved and grinned at the camera, and Johnson turned to the photographer. "Don't forget the candidate, young fellow," Johnson said with a grin. The crowd laughed, and Johnson held his Stetson high when the photographer turned his way.

A half-dozen local boys, two or three years younger than Tommy, hoisted themselves onto the tail of the helicopter and then slid around on the slick body, laughing and yelling.

By then, Robert Newsome had crawled out from under the collapsed canopy and was stretched out on a canvas lawn chair. His fat friend wiped at the old man's forehead with his wet handkerchief. Newsome lifted one arm and weakly waved to Johnson, but the congressman had pulled his reading glasses from his top pocket and started his speech.

He quickly ran through his notes, thanking the local business leaders and Democratic stalwarts by name. He moved past the opening niceties and on to his pet project, rural electrification, and then on to the need for more blacktop roads. He had just begun easing into the delicate issue of states' rights when his voice took on an edge and he glanced, distracted from his boilerplate speech, at the boys yelping and climbing on the helicopter, riding the tail like a horse, beating on it like a drum.

Suddenly Johnson stopped in mid-sentence. "Jumping Jehosaphat!" he said. "Where did these monkeys come from?" A nervous twitter ran through the crowd. The congressman glanced at the boys and wagged his head. "Where are these boys' folks?" he asked, stabbing a big finger at the crowd. Then he turned to the youngsters. "Boys," he said, unable to hide his impatience and annoyance any longer, "where in the world are your manners? Were you all raised in a zoo? Now skeedaddle!" he said with a forced grin, shooing them away with the sweep of his arm. He turned back to the crowd, with his arms out, palms up. "Can't somebody out there corral these kids?"

The spokesman interrupted Johnson then and started explaining in a falsely light-hearted manner how all sorts of strange things can happen when you fly around the state to be with the people. But by then Johnson had given up, and with a final wave and a grim smile retreated to the cabin where he sat, staring out the opposite way with his arms folded tight.

"Now you tell all your friends and neighbors," the aide hurriedly continued, "that you saw the next United States senator from the great state of Texas. And you tell them that it's time for a man with a platform, and that a vote for Lyndon Johnson . . ."

Just at that moment the congressman re-emerged from the cabin and again pushed the aide to one side. He had managed to put his blow-up with the boys behind him. "You tell your friends and neighbors not to vote for this man," Johnson said. He squinted into the crowd, his eyes promising some mischief, his confident grin now back.

He turned away from the gathering for a moment, and when he faced them again he threw his head back in an arrogant way, a distant, imperious look of disdain on his face. He clenched a corn cob pipe between his teeth. It was a perfect caricature of his opponent, Coke Stevenson.

The folks around the helicopter caught the joke at once,

and laughing and clapping and a couple of hisses rippled through the crowd.

"And boys," Johnson said, pointing the corn cob pipe at the youngsters still hanging around the helicopter. He patted the shiny, black aircraft, rubbed its smooth finish as if it were his favorite mare. "This machine is all that stands between me and defeat, and between you and having a pipe-puffing, hidebound United States senator. So if I get a little particular about this helicopter, it's because my future rides on it, and so does the future of this great state." He turned back to the crowd, still using the pipe to emphasize his point. "And perhaps, with me as your senator, even the nation's future depends on the powerful blades of this wonderful aircraft."

Johnson tossed the corncob pipe back in the cabin and an aide handed him his Stetson. He waved it all around to the clapping crowd and in a moment ducked back through the open door.

Suddenly the rotor started its whine and the blades began their slow whomping. By the time the helicopter lifted heavily into the air, most of the gathering had dispersed, men and women and screaming children scattering and scuttling to the shelter of their cars and trucks.

Tommy and Gene hung around, turning their backs to the helicopter when it lifted off, then eyeing it until it finally banked back to the east towards the country club where tonight's reception and dinner would be held.

The crew of men folded the canopy into a bulky bundle and wrestled the stakes around the landing area out of the sandy ground. Tommy watched the men, some of them shirtless now, as they worked, but he turned towards Gene when Grady straightened up from his job of coiling the rope, and stood there staring Tommy's way.

"Shit," Tommy whispered to his pal, "let's get out of here."

"Hey, what's wrong?" Gene asked, then quickly picked

up the look that Grady aimed their way. "Did he do this to you? Man, he's big as a grizzly bear. Why'd he pick on you?"

"I don't know," Tommy muttered, his head down.

"You got your car?" Gene asked.

"My bike."

"Me too. You want to go back to town?"

"I better go home. My daddy says I have to go with him and Mama tonight. To some grown-ups' party. Out at the country club. Man, maybe you could meet me out there. We could inspect that helicopter up close."

"Maybe," Gene said. "For a little while. If I don't have to work in town. It's all right? For me to go? I mean my daddy's not a member. Not of the country club. No way. But he is smoking the barbecue, so he'll be there."

"That's great, and sure, anybody can go," Tommy said. "They'll have lots more than just barbecue." He turned to leave and then, in the shade of a sycamore tree at the edge of the field he spotted Zoette. She just stood there as if she had been waiting for him and gave him a wave when he finally saw her.

"Is that Zoette?" Gene asked. He waved back. "Is she waving at me?"

"Who knows?" Tommy said. He waved back, too, then, and Zoette grinned and trotted across the field towards them.

"Aw, she grinned at you," Gene said. "You're not a candy-ass are you? You got the sweets for Zoette?"

Tommy blushed, his already blistered face turning a darker shade of red. "Look," he said. "I think there's something that Zoette wants to talk about. Something about school or something. Something–you know–sort of private." Shit, he thought. His words had left him, and he could hardly talk. Why didn't Gene just take a hint and leave?

"Man, I can't believe this," Gene said. "She's fifteen, a lot older than you are. She's got good tits and everything. What does she see in you?"

"I'm taking off," Tommy said. But instead of heading for his bicycle he moved out through the field, stepping around white-blossomed bull nettles, and met Zoette halfway.

"Don't do anything I wouldn't do," Gene yelled after him. "Jesus. Tommy Patterson and Zoette Acton. I never would have guessed it."

Tommy ignored Gene, figured he would finally go away if he didn't answer and didn't look back. He would catch a lot of teasing for this, but didn't care. He really didn't care.

Zoette stopped a couple of steps away from him. She frowned at his filthy blue shirt. Then looked up. "What happened to your face?" she asked. "It's all red." She shook her head and then she laughed. "You're not blushing, are you?"

"Got in a fight," Tommy said. He shrugged his shoulders and felt the sweaty shirt cling and stretch when he moved. "Sorry about my shirt. My mother's going to give me old Billy if she sees this."

"Who in the world did you fight?" Zoette asked, but didn't wait for an answer. "Your mama's not there. Not at your house," she said. "You'll beat her home if you're lucky."

Tommy looked at her as if she were a witch. "How do you know she isn't home?" he asked.

And Zoette told him, described how the Pattersons' Ford pulled up next to their trailer, and how Zoette was outside, hanging up clothes, and thought it was Tommy coming back. "I didn't know what you could want, but I started to run over to the car, and it wasn't you at all. I was so embarrassed."

"What's my mother doing out there? Did you talk to her?"

"I met her. She's a real lady, a pretty one, too. And, yeah, I met her, sort of."

"Was she shopping for furniture? Did she buy anything?" Tommy remembered Zoette saying that her daddy was always broke, and he hoped his mother had bought a table or something to help Mr. Acton out.

"We'll get chiggers out here," Zoette said. "And it's too hot in the sun. Come on." She led Tommy through the weeds to the Bermuda grass lawn, and the shade of one of the junior college's buildings. It was a rickety surplus barracks that the National Guard had donated for a classroom a year after the war had ended.

"You don't have a car, I guess," Zoette said.

Tommy shook his head. "My father won't let me drive his Buick, and my mother, well, you know she has the Ford. Maybe I can have it later, when she gets home." He felt awkward just standing there, and he was thirsty and dirty. "I only have my bike." Just admitting that made him feel like a grade school kid again.

He dreamed that he and Zoette were cruising around town, circling the Dairy King in his father's car. He could almost feel her sliding over next to him. He would tap the horn a couple of times at his buddies, and Zoette would punch the push buttons on the top of the radio that spelled BUICK and find just the right kind of music, something romantic.

He noticed a water hose coiled around a faucet at the end of the building. It was Saturday and no one was around, so he motioned to Zoette to follow him. He ran the water for a couple of minutes until it was cool to his hand, then offered it to Zoette. "You thirsty?" he asked. She nodded, and with one hand held her hair back and leaned forward while Tommy held the hose for her. She no longer had on the scoop-neck blouse, but a pink button-up-the-front shirt tucked into her white shorts. A wide white belt squeezed her waist.

After a minute she backed away, laughing and spluttering, trying to catch the rivulets of cool water that ran down her chin and neck and on to places that Tommy could not quite imagine.

It was his turn, and he gulped down the clear stream until

he felt he would burst, then ran the water over his face hoping to wash the redness away.

Zoette laughed when he finally lifted his head, letting the water run down his shirt. "You've got to wash that," she said. "It's so dirty I can't hardly stand it. You better not go home like that. Your mama will kill you, for sure."

"I can't wash it here," Tommy said. "It'll get my blue jeans all wet."

"Oh, don't be silly," Zoette. "You've got to take off your shirt. Don't worry. Just pretend we're going swimming out at Sand Springs. It's not a big deal." Sand Springs was a spring-fed pond out east of Cottonwood, a place with a pavilion and picnic tables, a place that Tommy's mother didn't like, afraid that he would get polio swimming there.

Tommy had learned how to swim at Sand Springs, anyway, when he was nine, and for a moment he remembered that feeling of lightness when he first pushed off the sandy bottom and floated. It had been like magic.

So Tommy imagined that he was out at Sand Springs now, and slipped out of the dirty shirt. He held it out wide at the shoulders while Zoette stuck her thumb over the end of the hose and sprayed it hard. He danced around while she sprayed, but his tennis shoes and socks got soaked. Tommy turned the shirt front and back, and then inside out, and pretty soon it looked almost clean again, but badly wrinkled.

"Here, let me have it," Zoette said. She wrung it out, twisting it hard, then shook the shirt until the most of the wrinkles fell out. She found a sunny patch of grass and spread the shirt carefully there, pulling and shaping it until she gave a satisfied nod. "It won't take long," she said. "Not in this heat."

Tommy unlaced his shoes and kicked them off. He pulled his socks off wrong side out and positioned them next to his shirt. They moved back in the shade of the barracks and sat so that their backs rested against the building.

They got quiet for a minute, and Tommy began to panic, trying to think of something clever to say. His mind felt empty. He picked at a sprout of Bermuda grass, pulling a seed stem free and nibbling at the white part at the base.

"So what did my mother buy?" Tommy finally asked. "I mean, did she get a table or something?"

Zoette looked at him, a funny expression on her face. She picked at a bump on her chin and Tommy wanted to tell her to stop, that a little blemish didn't bother him at all.

"Your mama wasn't after furniture, dummy," she said. "She came out for my mama to tell her fortune."

Tommy shook his head. "Uh-uh," he said. "There's no way my mother would ever do that. Daddy would let her have it, spending money on fortune telling. He even thinks all that religious stuff is a bunch of hocus-pocus."

Zoette shrugged. Hocus-pocus was her mama's religion. She stared at Tommy's bare chest, at the stringy, wet hairs that lay flat, and he wished he had fluffed them up. They looked thicker that way. He tensed his biceps as best he could without it being too apparent.

"Well, maybe it wasn't your mama," she said. "Just some lady who stole your Ford and drove it out there." She laughed. "It was her, Tommy. Believe me."

"Man," Tommy said. He tried to picture his mother in Zoette's trailer, what she would have done. "Does your mama have a crystal ball?" he asked. "Does it really work? Nobody knows the future, except maybe God. And my father says he's not so sure about that."

"Not a crystal ball, silly. That's from the movies. She reads cards and sometimes tea leaves, the way the leaves settle to the bottom of a cup means something. Mama knows. She has the gift. Even Daddy says so."

"What kind of cards?" Tommy asked.

"Well, not Old Maid," Zoette said. "And she nearly always reads palms. You can tell a lot from palms."

Tommy held up his hand and stared at it. His fingernails were dirty. A little streak of blood marked a scrape that he got scuffling with Grady.

"Here," Zoette said. "Let me see your hand. Reading palms is easy." She took Tommy's left hand and laid it palm up on her thigh. "Now hold your hand flat," she said.

Tommy felt his breath catch and he almost coughed, but was able to stifle it. He didn't want to do anything to break the spell of this moment. The back of his hand was actually, at that very moment, resting on Zoette's smooth, brown thigh. He couldn't believe he was so lucky.

"Now," she said. "Let me see." Zoette traced her finger up this line and then down that line on his palm. She had painted her fingernails dark red, and Tommy thought he could feel a wave of heat as her finger ran down the squiggly wrinkles of his palm. The charms on her silver bracelet danced across his wrist.

"See this," Zoette said, jabbing at the fat part of his palm. "This is the Mount of Luna. And here," she said, tracing a line towards his little finger. "This is the area of Mercury."

"What does all of that mean?" Tommy asked.

"Hold your horses," she said. "I'm getting to the good part." She pulled his hand up until it almost touched her breast and leaned close to him. Her lips were blood red. Two arcs of black mascara shadowed the fineness of her eyebrows. He wondered if she had a red sliding-top box of mascara on her dresser like his mother did. He tried to envision Zoette in her bedroom with the stiff little brush, stroking those fine dark hairs. She would be thinking about him all the while.

Tommy's hand began to shake and he tried to relax it, but when he did his fingers started to close. She pulled his hand back open.

"The life line is good–could be longer, but not bad. And this–you see this?" Tommy leaned over to look more closely, and their heads almost touched. He pulled back, just enough to study her. To his surprise, tiny red earrings pierced her ears. How had he missed them? His mother always said that he sleep-walked through the world, was always trying to get him to pay more attention. Maybe she was right.

Tommy stared at the sparkly jewels; he had never seen pierced ears before. His mother and all of the girls he knew wore clip-on earrings. Zoette was the most exotic girl he could ever imagine.

He leaned close again, and felt the springiness of her hair. Something sweet floated around her, honeysuckle or rose. Not sweet exactly. Maybe just the way pretty girls smelled.

She went on then, tracing Tommy's future with her slow movements, and he could see his life unfold on the pale skin of his hand as she talked. "You will obtain awareness at an early age," she said. She glanced over at him. A little of the lipstick smeared one tooth. "That might be good, and then it might not be good. I can't tell for sure. Mama would know."

"What does that mean? 'That I will obtain awareness at an early age?'" That didn't sound like Zoette at all, but something that she was reading.

"Oh, you know. It means that you were born an old person. That you know things early that mostly older people would know."

Oh, God. Tommy thought. Is Zoette talking about sex and stuff? Is she hinting for me to try something? "Wouldn't that be a bad thing?" Tommy asked. "What would it help to be an old person when you're not really old?"

Zoette shrugged. "It doesn't matter," she said. "There's nothing you can do about it." She folded up his fingers and pushed his hand away.

"Wow," Tommy said. "Is that it? I mean is there anything there about playing basketball or football?"

"No, silly." Zoette scrambled to her feet. She checked out Tommy's shirt, drying in the sun. "Not bad," she said, holding it up and shaking it out. "Dry enough to wear." She tossed it to Tommy.

"Well," she said. "I've got to go."

This was like before, when Tommy had driven her home in the Ford. Zoette had been warm and friendly and then she just turned it off and acted as if she didn't like him–not even a little.

"Yeah, well me, too." Tommy pulled on his shirt and buttoned it while he got to his feet. He brushed at his jeans, but they were pretty hopeless. "I've got to go with my parents tonight," he said. "To some dumb party out at the country club. It's about politics and stuff. I don't see why I have to go."

"Yeah," Zoette said. "Well, I wish I could go to the country club. I wish my parents would take me to a party there."

She seemed a little angry, as if she blamed Tommy for the way her family was. Golly, he thought, girls sure aren't easy to understand.

In the distance between two puffy summer clouds, Tommy thought he spotted the helicopter headed back towards them, but it was only a turkey buzzard above the tree line, tilting its wings.

"How will you get home?" Tommy asked.

"Same way I got here," she said. "It's not hard to catch a ride."

"Yeah, I guess not," Tommy said. He felt desperate, imagining some older guy, maybe a junior or senior, stopping to pick up Zoette. An older guy would know lots of stuff to talk about when he drove her home.

And oh damn! Before he let her out, would she slide over next to him and put her hand on his thigh and kiss him, too? "I can give you a ride on my bike," Tommy said. "I mean, I know it's not the same as a car, but I could get you back to town, anyway."

Zoette turned her head to one side the way a cardinal does before it pecks at a seed. "You're sweet," she said. She shook her head. "I'll just cut across the field–it isn't far to town."

"Maybe you could come to the reception at the country club tonight. It starts early, and nobody will check or anything. Everybody in town is invited. There's supposed to be a bunch of barbecue. And a band from the Fiddlers' Contest will be playing."

"I heard that sometimes they get drunk at those parties," Zoette said, "and couples go swimming in the pool. You know, skinny-dipping. And they're not always married to each other, either."

Tommy hadn't heard that. But he knew his parents stayed away from the country club crowd for some reason. He had thought it was because his father considered golf "a useless sport," and that the club in the basement was "a retreat for all the drunks in town."

Tommy had wanted to caddy there on weekends–you could make fifty cents carrying a bag for nine holes–but his father wouldn't allow it. "That bunch is one step up from white trash," Thomas said. "With more money than brains."

Now Tommy understood. It wasn't the golf, or even the drinking in the basement that kept his parents away. It was those midnight skinny-dips. Maybe he would hang around the pool if the party ran late. Maybe he would catch some of those ladies naked in the pool.

"If I could get there," Zoette said, "would you give me a ride back home? I don't like to be on the road by myself at night. Not after what happened to Corrine Abernathy."

"A ride?" Tommy figured his family would ride out together in the Buick. For some reason all being together was important to his mother. But maybe he could come up with some excuse to take the Ford. "Sure," he said. "I can give you a ride home. I think so."

"Don't 'think so,' Tommy. I need to know. Or I'm not going."

"Well, sure, then," he said. If he had to slip out of the party and run all the way back home for the Ford he would do it. "It'll be easy. You can count on me."

"A party. At the country club. And not with a bunch of kids." She reached over and touched Tommy's arm. "I mean you're not really a kid. Remember your fortune? You will obtain awareness at an early age. See, already you're not a kid."

And just like that, Zoette stepped back and blew him a kiss. Before Tommy could react she turned and trotted away across the field, sidestepping the bull nettles and briars. Without even a glance back, she was gone. ❖

Chapter Ten

Thomas parked the Buick once again at the rear of his office, this time where a neighbor's red oak tree would shade his car by mid-afternoon, according to his calculations. He glanced at his watch; it was two-thirty. He had almost three hours to prepare his strategy for this evening's reception.

The music–if one was generous enough to call it that–screeched and squawked from downtown louder than before, and Thomas entered the calm and orderliness of his office with relief. It was stuffy inside and normally he would have opened the windows to the spring breeze. But not today. He switched on an oscillating fan in the corner of the room. The whir of warm air did little to help, but the heat was more bearable than the ruckus from the courthouse square.

He would sit at Belinda's desk while he ate the meatloaf sandwich. First he wiped the surface down with a couple of folded tissues, accumulating a few stray blondish hairs and a smattering of white powder and some unidentifiable crumbs. The white powder wasn't make-up, not with Belinda. Probably from the powdered sugar donuts she sneaked from the bottom drawer of her desk.

Thomas didn't ask much of Belinda, and to clean her desk before she left for the day didn't seem unreasonable. He provided the furniture polish and rags and glass cleaner–they were in the storage closet. Why she refused to use them, he couldn't understand. It seemed like a small thing to leave the top of the desk polished and her in-basket empty.

He settled into Belinda's chair and inspected his sandwich, pulling up one corner of the white bread, then turning the sandwich over and checking the other side. He felt slightly–and strangely–disappointed when he found Mary Lee's preparation to be flawless. A thin spread of salad dressing on the top slice of bread and a generous smear of ketchup on the bottom slice. He took a bite. The ketchuped slice of bread was a little soggy. "Oh, well," he muttered, and hurried through his lunch, eager to get on with his strategy planning.

By reputation Congressman Johnson was a forceful and strong-willed man, especially formidable in nose-to-nose confrontations. So Thomas concluded that he wouldn't be able to logically convince the man that throwing his support behind Thomas Patterson for state district judge would be an advantageous move. But every man had his weakness, and Johnson, again by way of rumor and newspaper reports, harbored a mammoth ego. And over-sized egos could be swayed by what they most needed–flattery and adulation.

Most of Cottonwood's residents–especially the professionals that he dealt with day to day–would not have described Thomas as wily. And, truth be told, Thomas was not overly fond of viewing himself in that way. Wily came weighted with mostly negative connotations. But so did clever and cunning and shrewd. Oh, well. Those were only words.

So flattery as a start, as a way to get the congressman's attention and keep it. For Thomas knew others would be there fawning over the candidate, wanting to bask in the little bit of reflected light that Johnson would allow to escape. Robert Newsome would be the biggest obstacle. For Newsome, wily was hardly a strong enough word. He had persevered as the county's Democratic chairman for untold years by being wily. There were foxes that would do well to sit at his feet.

Lyndon Johnson's endorsement of Thomas must have the appearance of boosting the congressman in his race with Coke Stevenson. That was a given, for all of Johnson's energy would be aimed towards that end. So Thomas had to show that he was the opposite of a corn-cob-pipe-smoking, dyed-in-the-wool Dixiecrat. That he was a progressive along the lines of former Texas Governor Dan Moody. Or maybe he would be better off not to drop names at all. Who could know what prejudices and grudges the congressman held. Thomas would play it safe.

A roar from overhead startled Thomas out of his concentration. He hurried to the back door and scanning the sky moved out onto the pea gravel of the parking lot. The roar subsided, but an eerie silence settled over the town, and now, for a few moments this might have been an ordinary Saturday in May, and not Old Fiddlers' Contest day at all, for the fiddling and screeching and yodcling had stopped. And then in the distance the roar of an engine came to him again, and before he knew it a huge black helicopter soared so low overhead that the leaves of the red oak tree stirred and a few of last fall's acorns pinged the top of the Buick. This time around a voice boomed out of the sky, "This is Lyndon Johnson, your next United States senator from the great state of Texas."

Thomas lifted his arms to the sky. "Bravo," he yelled at the helicopter, not knowing exactly what was appropriate to yell. Oh, he's a daredevil for certain, Thomas thought. A risk taker. Well, perhaps Johnson is just the man to take a chance on me.

It was now almost four, and as Thomas moved back inside, he mentally allocated himself one hour more to complete his list of alternate stratagems. He settled back at his desk, with three freshly sharpened #2-1/2 yellow pencils lined up to one side.

The front door of the building slowly opened–Thomas could not see it from his interior office, and he did not hear it, but a breeze pushed through the building and fluttered the papers on his desk. "Who's there," he asked, not moving. "Can I help you?" He removed his reading glasses and dropped them in his shirt pocket.

"Mr. Patterson. Are you here?" The voice was timid and wispy, but he recognized at once that it was Belinda.

"Belinda? Is that you?" Thomas pushed back from his desk and moved to the front room. His secretary stood there, an odd look on her face–a frightened look, Thomas quickly ascertained–and it appeared she had been crying, her face patterned with odd-shaped splotches. She was not alone. Behind her, straw hat in hand, stood her dour looking husband, Douglas Donohoo.

"Come in, come in," Thomas said, and the couple cautiously stepped inside. Douglas glanced back towards the street, before closing the door behind them.

"It's Saturday, Belinda. Isn't it? What in the world are you doing here?" And for a moment Thomas felt disoriented, as if he had his days mixed up. Perhaps this was Monday and the Saturday he had believed it to be was only a dark dream of his wild imaginings.

Belinda nodded. Her glasses slid down her nose a little, and she removed them. Her eyes were puffy and red, but her long hair was in its usual braided and twisted bun.

"Now I'll get right to the point, Mr. Patterson." Douglas stepped forward. He appeared to have just come from his welding shop, for his face was blistered and his hair wet and slicked back as if he had only minutes before cleaned up to make this call. Old burn scars streaked his freckled arms. A pair of gripping pliers hung from the side loop of his overalls. He wore badly scuffed steel-toed work boots.

"Belinda can't work here no more," he said. "We had them phone calls all night, foul-mouthed calls they were. They was about you," he said. "You and that nigger Carroll. Calling you and that boy names that the Lord would strike me dead for repeating."

Belinda stared at the floor and dug into her purse for a tissue.

"They–whoever made those phone calls–threatened you? Not to work for me? Why that's preposterous." Thomas strode to the front window and parted the curtains. "Did you call Sheriff Sweeten? Now there's a man who could straighten this out. He would put those hoodlums in their places."

"It's safer for Belinda just to quit," Douglas said. He turned to Belinda and she nodded. "We just don't want no trouble, Mr. Patterson."

"Well, it's trouble for me," Thomas said. "A good secretary is not that easy to come by, and I pay a fair salary, and anyone else would have to be trained. Oh, yes. It is more than a bit of trouble for me, Mr. Donohoo."

Now don't panic, Thomas told himself. He glanced at the calendar on the wall. The May picture glowed above the dates, a fisherman at sunrise, wading in a sparkling, mountain trout stream, his fly rod in hand.

"I know," he finally said. The calendar had provided the inspiration. "A vacation. Two weeks off, Belinda. In that time I will guarantee you that this is a dead issue. That it will be only an unpleasant and fading memory." He pointed his finger at Douglas and the big man took a half-step back.

"It will go away because by tomorrow I can almost assure you that I will have one of the most powerful men in the state of Texas endorse me, and endorse my record, publicly, in the state's newspapers. And then no one–not the stubborn remains of the Klan and not a bunch of ignorant thugs–will dare do anything to harm me, or any of those around me. On this you have my word."

Belinda looked at her husband. He gave her a what-do-you-think look back, and she shrugged. "Whatever you think," she said.

"A paid vacation," Douglas said. "Two weeks. And Belinda won't have to make up for it later. She don't work Saturdays. But you already know that."

"You have my word," Thomas said.

The couple nodded.

Thomas went to the calendar and marked an X on Monday, June 13. "Maybe I'll take some time off, too. Take the family down to the coast. Or maybe to the mountains this year. Do some trout fishing."

But the Donohoos were already out the door, checking both ways before hurrying to their car that was parked out front. In a minute they pulled away from the curb and made a U-turn that headed them away from downtown.

At precisely five o'clock Thomas slipped back into his suit coat and tightened the tie he had loosened while he worked. He checked that the windows and doors were secured, then briskly walked towards his car. He felt good about the way he had handled the bizarre incident with the Donohoos. Reason and logic and calm always prevailed.

As he approached the Buick, he noticed the shade from the red oak tree had crept across the car, just as Thomas had calculated that it would, and he smiled. A satisfied smile.

A stake-bed truck had parked on the edge of Thomas's parking lot. An infringement, but those things happened on this one, most crowded day of the year, and Thomas would overlook it. The cab of the truck was dented and scratched from too many trips hauling fence posts down out of those sorry cedar hills east of Cottonwood, from places like Larue and Fincastle.

The bed of the truck was empty except for a couple of double bit axes secured to the side of a wooden tool chest. A mongrel hound of many colors sprawled across the top of the tool chest, and he barked once–not an unfriendly bark–when Thomas walked by. A couple of men in beat-up hats slouched down in the front. Thomas glanced their way and nodded–one of the expected courtesies in a small town, even if the two were rough looking strangers. One of them nodded back and spit a dog-turd sized wad of tobacco out the window Thomas's way. The truck sputtered to life and one of the men gave out a ridiculous yell. The driver laughed and dangled his arm out the window, beating the truck door like a tom-tom, and they roared off trailing a haze of smoke.

Thomas figured they had been at the fiddlers' contest, and probably were liquored-up from a Mason jar of home brew. Oh, well, he thought, even the simpletons have to have their day.

Without really looking Thomas grasped the Buick's door handle, then jerked his hand back. The chrome handle was smeared with something, something foul. And then he smelled the dog shit. He spun around, hoping to catch sight of the truck, to get the license number if he could. But it was gone. "Damn you," he said. "Damn you to hell!"

He looked around the parking lot, hoping to spot even a scrap of newspaper trapped against the fence to wipe his hand on. He would have to go back in the office to wash, but his keys were in his right trousers pocket and he struggled, holding his filthy, stinking right hand in the air, while trying to snare the keys with his left hand. The effort turned him in a circle and he spun around for a minute before he was able to finally grasp the ring of keys.

It was simple enough to wash the dog shit off his hands, but the smell just wouldn't fade away. Thomas washed and dried and sniffed his hands over and over, before giving up. His hands were clean, and he figured the odor must be from some of the dog shit that he had inhaled into his nostrils.

In the parking lot he moved all around the Buick, afraid that he would find more serious mischief done.

Finally satisfied, he decided to avoid the shit-smeared car handle all together, and use the passenger door and slide across. Now he was running late, and worried that Mary Lee might lose track of time and not start her multitude of preparations for the night until he arrived.

Thomas checked around one last time to make sure that the truck hadn't circled back while he had washed up. It was all clear. With relief he sank into the car, and slammed the door. His shoes slid across something on the floorboard, something firm and rubbery, and he glanced down to see the coil of a snake, a water moccasin as big around as his forearm. Thomas yelled, the sound a desperate exhalation of breath, one that emptied his lungs. An awakening from a nightmare sort of sound.

Afterwards, he could not remember bolting from the car, but he had, stumbling and then crawling away, where he stopped, trying to regain his breath. He felt his ankles, his legs. He was afraid the snake had struck him and that his legs had gone numb. He could almost feel the venom creeping towards his hammering heart.

He pulled up his trousers legs, but could find nothing, just a trace of a scrape on his shin. The snake had not struck. It had not even moved. It must be dead. Another trick from the cedar choppers.

Thomas stood and dusted himself off. He found a fallen sycamore branch and poked at the snake, finally lifting it gingerly out the door, and tossing it into the weeds.

The bastards, he thought. The dirty bastards. He forgave himself for his language–the severity of their trick deserved even stronger language than that. But bastards would have to do, and he repeated it over and over as he raced the Buick home, feeling better, stronger all the while. He would show those dirty bastards, he thought. All of them. ❖

Chapter Eleven

The session with Madame Acton passed like a dream, Mary Lee losing all sense of place and time. She seemed to float, move out of her old Mary Lee self, transformed into a spectator of the story of her own life. The tea leaves drifted into their inevitable, preordained places in the cup. The Tarot card figures danced and grimaced and cavorted and combined to uniquely and resolutely define both past and future.

Driving back to town Mary Lee held her left hand in her lap, using only the fingers of that hand to touch the steering wheel when it was absolutely necessary. For the palm of that hand still tingled from the tracings of Madame Acton's finger, the crimson fingernail finding every hidden crease and wrinkle and bump and mound.

The gas gauge was on empty. Tommy never put more than a dollar's worth of gas in, and Mary Lee had driven farther than she had planned. She pulled into the Magnolia station and tapped her fingers on the steering wheel. It was almost five. Thomas would be home any minute, upset that she wasn't there.

A pimply-faced boy shuffled out to the car. "Fill 'er up?" he asked, and Mary Lee nodded. "Please hurry," she said, and the boy grinned. "Gas pump's halfway on the blink," he said. "Nothin' I can do about that."

While the tank slowly filled, the boy wiped the windows all around with a ragged chamois. Yellow and orange remains of unidentifiable grasshoppers and butterflies speckled the front windshield and smeared under the pressure of the chamois. Mary Lee looked away.

Just as he was topping off the tank, a Ford coupe carrying two men pulled in behind Mary Lee.

She glanced in the rearview mirror. The car was new, its shiny green finish glistened in the sun. She recognized the driver at once, the way he appeared to be stuffed into the little Ford. Oh, damn, she thought. It's that big-mouth Coach Green. And double damn! Just her luck. The other fellow that show-off Vernon Paroline, the Ford dealer.

Mary Lee was thankful that Thomas had driven up to Dallas for his Buick, a move that put the Pattersons a notch above the locals who had no option but to buy their cars from Paroline Ford.

Vernon eased out of the coupe, and adjusted his suspenders. He tossed his cigarette to the pavement and smeared it with his toe. He was a sharp dresser, Mary Lee had to admit. His shirt with bold yellow stripes and his tan gabardine suit, his tan and white wing-tip shoes.

He cocked his straw hat at just the right angle and wiped the toe of each shoe on the back of the opposite pants leg. A silly dance to Mary Lee. Vernon moved to her side of the car and nodded, then tilted his hat back on his head. "Mary Lee," he said with a grin. He looked the car up and down. "About time for a new Ford," he said. "A lady like you shouldn't be driving around town in one this old." He pulled back. " A '39 model. Right?"

"You know perfectly well what model this is, Vernon Paroline." She looked up at him, shading her eyes with one hand. Clouds hurried by the flying red horse on the Magnolia station's roof and made it appear to sail by. "And we don't need a new Ford as long as this one serves as reliable transportation."

Coach Joe Mack Green, wearing a pair of dark green aviator glasses swung out of the coupe just then and propped himself on the open door, watching and listening.

"Well, now. I reckon not," Vernon said. "You and that lawyer husband was always prudent. Up 'til now." He leaned down, close to Mary Lee, as if he was inspecting the car's interior. Nicotine had yellowed his teeth. His eyes moved all around. She felt them pass from her breasts to her legs. "Well, everything here seems to be in fine shape," he said. "Yeah, mighty fine shape."

Mary Lee touched the top button on her print dress and checked to see that the hem covered her knees.

"You and the hubby going out to the club tonight?" Vernon asked. "For the big shindig? I hear that Johnson fellow can be mighty entertaining."

"It all depends," Mary Lee said. She knew Vernon and his wife Rita would be there. Shindig or not, they would be at the country club until midnight. Mary Lee had heard stories. Her friend Kate knew the dirt on those two.

"Depends on what?" Vernon asked. He grinned a smart-alecky grin. "Whether that lawyer husband of yours is too chicken to show his face."

"Now, Vernon Paroline. What in the world in this town could scare Thomas? Nothing. That's what. Chicken my eye." But Vernon's question had unsettled Mary Lee.

"Coach Green, there, tells me different." He gestured towards the shiny green coupe with his chin. "Trouble might be brewing, the man says. The nigra problem that Thomas goggle-headed us into has some folks all worked up. That's what the coach tells me, anyhow."

He straightened up and held his hands out in an innocent gesture. "For sure I don't know."

The boy finished with the gas and moved towards Mary Lee, holding out a charge ticket for her to sign. She started the engine and scrawled her name.

Vernon leaned towards her again, his arms resting on

the top of the car. Mary Lee pulled back from his cigarette breath. "Maybe I'll ask you for a dance tonight–if you show up, that is."

"Oh, we will show up, Vernon. You can bet on that. The congressman and Thomas have a special–a very close–relationship." A little fib, when it anticipated the truth to come, never hurt a thing. "And you can ask me to dance if you like. And I will tell you no."

"Don't know what you might be missing," Vernon said, that stupid grin still on his face. "Maybe with the coach then. He'll be there, and he's quick on his feet."

"I'd rather dance with a man who is a little less quick on his feet," Mary Lee said, "and a little bit quicker up here, thank you," and she tapped the side of her head with one finger.

Vernon laughed and stepped back as the car shot forward, and in a moment Mary Lee whipped the Ford out onto the street and sped away.

When she discreetly glanced back in the rearview mirror Vernon lifted his hat and swept it in front of him in an exaggerated bow.

That encounter with Vernon Paroline had broken Madame Acton's spell, and now, hurrying back home, Mary Lee could hardly recall the advice she had offered, or the future that the woman had so clearly pointed out. Then she remembered. "Temptation, change, and someone to show you the way." Well, Mary Lee didn't know about the first two, but the third–the someone to show the way–that had to be Congressman Johnson, and this would be the night. ❖

Chapter Twelve

It was after five-thirty when Thomas finally swung the Buick into the driveway at home. The Ford appeared to be safely parked out front, but Thomas had an impulse to check the door handles, to see if they had been defiled. But no, he wouldn't be drawn into that game with those hillbilly ignoramuses.

He hurried to the house, taking the porch steps two at a time. In the best of worlds Mary Lee would have his light blue suit laid out on the bed. He would wear his red and blue tie–bold, yet in good taste. After he showered and shaved he would retreat to the living room for a few minutes of quiet in order to collect his thoughts once again. The incident with the dog shit and the roughness of those two cedar choppers had side-swiped him, and he needed time to compose himself before the reception.

He resolved not to say one word of the afternoon's unpleasantness to Mary Lee. This Chester Carroll ordeal was one that he could handle, but to introduce Mary Lee into the incident's fallout would create a state of havoc. He could not stand that.

"Time heals all things," he said quietly. A ridiculous cliché that Adelle spouted in her times of distress. How that popped into his head he didn't know. But things would work out. Belinda would be at her desk at eight a.m. two weeks from Monday–Thomas knew that the Donohoos needed her wages–and the country yokels with their mad-dog surliness would retreat back into the cedar hills.

A period of normality would set in, and Thomas could get back to the business at hand. Tonight would be a start–a remarkably quick start–on that process.

He found Mary Lee in the bedroom, moving back and forth in a strange manner between the closet and bathroom. Her hair dangled in wide strands, the ends wrapped around cylinders as big as tin cans that swung like pendulums when she moved. From the living room the phonograph blared at top volume. It was Dinah Shore crooning that scratchy "Gypsy" song, and Mary Lee, before she noticed Thomas waiting there, appeared to be dancing.

"My suit," Thomas said, hurrying towards the closet, as if he hadn't caught Mary Lee gliding and pirouetting across the smooth floor.

"My blue summer suit. The only decent summer suit I own. I certainly hope it's clean. It may need pressing. I assumed that you would have already seen to this. I have more important things on my mind, you know."

Finally he turned to look directly at his wife. Mary Lee appeared to be flustered, but swung around to hold up her new green dress, swaying just a little, as if to show Thomas that she had not been dancing at all, but simply shaking the wrinkles out of her dress.

Thomas ignored that useless ploy. She had been dancing alone in the house, and he had caught her red-handed. Red-handed wasn't quite the right allusion, he knew. But he had caught her anyway, dancing to that infernal gypsy song. He stared blankly into the closet. "I have strategies to implement. Strategies, that if they are successful, will change my fortunes. And that, as you know, means our fortunes. I don't need to be worrying about the state of my blue summer suit."

The last of the song died out in the living room. Thank God, Mary Lee thought. Now I can ignore that. For she knew that Thomas would never bring up, or ask her to explain something as embarrassing and intimate as her dancing alone in their bedroom.

The front door slammed. That would be Tommy. Mary Lee heard him open the refrigerator, and the milk jug clunk on the tile counter. She could visualize Tommy pouring too much chocolate syrup in the glass, followed by the milk. The chocolate syrup would run down the side of can, then slowly congeal on the rack in the refrigerator. There would be a circle of chocolate on the counter top and the floor would be sticky from dribbled milk. Then came the whirl of an iced tea spoon and the stirring of the chocolate into the milk went on forever. Boys were only messy men in process.

"Thomas," she said. "Your blue suit is clean and it is pressed. It is on a wooden hanger on the hook behind the closet door." She pulled her hair free from the tin cylinders and shook her head, running her fingers through her hair. She tried to remember what Madame Acton had told her–something about the rewards that would come with patience and perseverance. Well, Madame Acton didn't know Thomas. But Mary Lee would try.

"You poor dear," she said. "I know that you are worried about this evening. But don't be agitated. Everything will go just fine."

"I am not agitated!" Thomas said, lifting the suit coat from the hanger and laying it carefully across the bed. "And everything may not go just fine. Oh, how I hate that expression. That's what they say in Tyler. What they say in Cottonwood, but we never would have said that in Dallas. Just fine in a pig's eye!"

At that moment Tommy appeared at the open bedroom door. He held the glass to his lips, tilted back as far as possible while he waited for the last trickle of the chocolate syrup to reach his tongue. He pulled the glass back down at Thomas's "Just fine in a pig's eye" statement, and started to back out of the room.

"What in the world happened to you, young man?" Mary Lee eyed him up and down.

Tommy had thought he looked okay now, after washing his shirt. Zoette had said so. He stared out the window, concentrating on the push lawn mower that leaned against the fence.

He had forgotten to roll it to the garage yesterday when he mowed the yard, and if it got rained on his father would give him holy-what-for for sure. He pulled the front of his shirt out and inspected it.

"I was at the fair grounds–the junior college–when the helicopter came in. Man, it was huge. And black. I thought it would be green. I was all sweaty since I didn't have the car and had to ride my bike out there." He paused, hoping that his parents would understand now the importance of him always having a car. "And the helicopter circled around, high at first, and then lower and lower. Finally it stopped and hovered right over our heads. And man, that Mr. Johnson–he's a daredevil for sure–he leaned right out and waved, speaking right at us through a speaker they had rigged up, and then they got so low that the blades whipped everything up. I mean dirt and bull nettles and leaves and everything. All over everybody." He laughed. "Most everybody hightailed it out of there then, and I started to back off, but that stuff all stuck to my shirt, anyway. And then I got a hose and tried to clean up, but, anyway . . ." Tommy took a deep breath. "And all that sand," he said, touching his cheeks, must have chapped my face." He hoped he had covered everything.

"Okay, okay son," Thomas said. "That's enough. Now go get cleaned up. You need to shower and . . ." He looked closer at his son. "Come here."

Tommy stepped towards his father. "You need a razor. Those hairs on your chin. They won't do. Listen. You're becoming a man so you have to learn the ways of a man. When I have time," he said, catching Mary Lee's eye. "We need to have a talk. A man-to-man talk." Thomas dismissed his son with a wave of his hand. "But not now. Not today. Now go on. We will leave within an hour."

"Okay," Tommy said. "But I wondered if it would be all right if I took the Ford tonight. You know, it gets awful boring for me at those receptions. I mean I can be there with you for a while, but after we eat I might want to come back home."

"Not 'awful' boring, son," Thomas said. "Awfully–if you have to use that word. Awfully boring."

Tommy fought off his urge to roll his eyes.

"Why wouldn't you like to stay at the party?" Mary Lee said. "Some kids your age, maybe some of your friends, will be there, I would think."

"Oh, I doubt it," Tommy said. He stared at the floor. "Their parents won't make them go. And I've been on the move all day long. I might want to listen to the radio and turn in early."

Mary Lee shot Thomas one of her "Now do you see?" glances.

Thomas lifted his hand for silence and peace. "Please," he said. "This issue is not worth the effort. Yes, you may take the Ford. But no, I want you to stay around for a while–not just for dinner. I want you to meet Congressman Johnson. Be thinking what you will say to him. Have a forceful handshake. Look him straight in the eye. Let him see what kind of stock the Pattersons come from."

"Oh, Thomas," Mary Lee said. "He's only a boy."

"Your inconsistencies drive me crazy." Thomas shook his head. "Now, please, we must get ready to go."

As Tommy backed out of the room there was a knock at the front door. Three soft knocks. Tommy turned to go, but Thomas stopped him. "No, son. Let me get it." His mind flashed to the no-good cedar choppers outside the office. They might have come to the house trying to stir up things some more.

But it wasn't the two cedar choppers at all. Through the glass of the front door window with its gauzy curtain he could make out Odie Mae Harwood, their neighbor from next door. Oh Lord, Thomas thought. What have I done to deserve this? But he opened the door and nodded with a forced smile.

Right away, as if Thomas had hit some invisible switch, Odie Mae started talking in a stream that wouldn't stop, one that appeared to have been building for quite a while. "Now last week your wife told me, right across that fence out back, that my cats were feral. 'Feral,' she said. 'Now you mean wild?' I said. I don't think she knew what she meant."

Thomas checked his watch, and glanced back over his shoulder. Where in the world was Mary Lee when he needed her? He held up his hand, trying to interrupt, but Odie Mae ignored him.

"My cats are not feral, and they are not wild. They are outdoor cats, and a whole lot better off than if I had them cooped up inside all day and night. Wild cats don't have names–that's how you tell the difference–and I know ever' one of them cats by first name." She started to name them, "Fluffy and Tom and Mustard and String Bean," but Thomas retreated down the entrance hall, yelling for Mary Lee to come help.

By the time the two of them got back, Odie Mae was stuck. "I'm trying to remember that calico's name. I will, if you'll give me a minute."

"Odie Mae," Mary Lee said. Her voice got unnaturally sweet when she talked to old ladies–an affectation that Thomas hated. "I understand about the cats. I was confused, but not any more."

"Circle. That's the calico's name." Odie Mae nodded and beamed. "She's always chasing her tail."

"Now let's see," Odie Mae said. "There was something else. Something important. Oh, yes. Now I remember. A couple of fellows came to my door. They had been over here, out on your front walk, helloing the house. I watched them through my side curtain. One of them big old boys went around back, helloing from there."

"They were big men," Thomas asked. "In overalls?"

Odie Mae nodded. “Then they decided to try my place, but I ducked down and kept quiet and after a while they took off in their truck, swerving down the street so that I thought they’d lose their hound dog off the back.”

“Oh, my God,” Thomas said. He stepped out on the porch and checked the street both ways. He hoped those two had finally passed out from the moonshine.

He thanked Odie Mae, shutting the door almost in her face.

“Some people,” she muttered and hobbled back down the steps.

“What in the world was that all about,” Mary Lee asked.

“Oh, a couple of brothers, threatening to sue a nephew for carrying off some cedar posts. Something like that. If they come back around ignore them. And don’t even go to the door. They’re just a pair of ignorant trouble makers.” ❖

Chapter Thirteen

Cottonwood Country Club lay at the south edge of town, its entrance marked by a double row of yellow-needled pine trees that would have thrived thirty miles farther east where the soil was less alkaline. Until a two years before, a local oil man owned those rolling, sandy hills, and before his untimely death had dammed up a couple of draws for small lakes. There he built the shell of what was designed to be his dream house.

His widow sold the property to a local group of businessmen who solicited memberships to turn the not yet finished country estate into a country club with a nine-hole golf course.

The oilman had dreamed of a mansion–a mansion for that part of Texas–and the main house stood three stories high on the rise of a hill. The walls were constructed of iron ore rocks trucked in from the hilly east end of the county, and the would-be mansion took on the dark and ancient appearance of a medieval castle.

They converted the lower floor into the pro shop and the kitchen, and enclosed a separate bar that held a couple of pool tables–the bar accessible only from an entrance in the back.

Wide rock steps led up to the second, or main floor, creating a grand entrance into the Red Room–its walls gaudy with red flocked wallpaper–where most parties were held. The dining room with a dumb waiter to connect it with the kitchen below took up the rest of that floor. An extended, rock-walled veranda ran the length of the Red Room and provided a view of the golf course and the farm country that stretched to the south.

The bedrooms on the third floor were converted into two guest suites, available for the members' out of town visitors. Or, as was the case on this Saturday night, for visiting dignitaries such as Congressman Lyndon Johnson.

By seven, when the Patterson procession passed under the rainbow-shaped arch at the entrance to the country club, a few dozen cars already packed the graveled lot.

"There'll be no place to park," Thomas said. He glanced in the Buick's rearview mirror at Tommy, who was keeping the Ford a safe distance behind. "By now old Newsome will have the congressman cornered and be feeding him a line of baloney."

"I doubt that Lyndon Johnson will give the time of day to that old man," Mary Lee said. She patted the curls of her up-do, not quite happy with how they fluffed down over her forehead. She pulled the rearview mirror of the Buick around and dabbed her lips with one last layer of "Surprise." She blotted them on a tissue and tucked the red, bullet shaped case back into her rhinestone patterned purse.

Thomas jerked the rearview mirror back "I need to keep my eye on the boy," he said. "If he parks at the edge of the road some tipsy driver might sideswipe the car. You can't tell how long some of them have hung out here in the bar. I tried to get Sheriff Sweeten to monitor the place, but he's not about to touch those country club types."

"Oh, Thomas," Mary Lee sighed. "Just let Tommy be, won't you? Nobody's going to hit the Ford. It's ancient. And, anyway, we could use a newer one." She started to say, "That's what Vernon Paroline told me," but thought better of it. This was not the right moment to agitate Thomas.

Mary Lee checked her green satin pumps–they were lovely–but now her nylons seemed a little too dark at the shoes' open toes. She hoped that Kate would be there. She might have an extra pair of nylons in her purse. And Kate could check the seams that ran down the backs of her legs.

Thomas finally found an open place to park, but after a moment's hesitation, eased on by. "What was wrong with that spot?" Mary Lee said. "I don't want to walk forever across that gravel. It will ruin my shoes."

Thomas circled back around and pulled up as close as he could to the edge of the rock walk that led to the stairs. Tommy was already there, waiting.

"He looks so nice," Mary Lee said. "All dressed up in a jacket and a tie."

"He's wearing white socks," Thomas said. "I can't believe you let our son wear white socks with his black dress slacks."

"'Let?'" Mary Lee said. 'Let?' I didn't let him do anything. Why didn't you notice them earlier?"

"Okay, okay," Thomas said. "Please. I'll meet you upstairs. I'll park the car and take a couple of minutes to compose myself. If I possibly can."

"You possibly can't," Mary Lee muttered. "No, Tommy and I will wait for you. Here on the walk. We will make our entrance together." She pushed the door open and swung her legs out. The toes of her nylons looked better in the natural light.

Thomas parked the Buick and hurried back to where Mary Lee and Tommy waited. The sun was beginning to set behind him, and in the last glow of the evening, Thomas tried to fight–or keep from embracing–a general malaise that seemed to have overtaken him.

When he glanced up at his wife, waiting for him on the rock steps with Tommy, he was suddenly overcome by her presence. It wasn't her beauty, for Mary Lee–although attractive enough–did not possess the classic features of beauty. It wasn't her new green dress with its sweetheart neckline, or her hair that swept up behind her head, held in place by a single jeweled barrette that glittered when she turned. He caught its gleam even from that distance away. But at thirty-seven she was striking, had not gone the way of so many women of her age, thickening out and drooping down. Thomas chastised himself for not being more appreciative.

Mary Lee might have been some other man's wife, and he stopped and stared at her for a moment, as if for the first time, not convinced that he had ever truly known her.

That dress must have cost a pretty penny, he thought, not comfortable with where his mind had wandered. That Kate Crowder doesn't run a bargain basement, for certain.

The helicopter sat tethered out to his right, a short distance from the club house. It seemed to crouch there like a huge dirt dauber, ready to spin into the air. Thomas tried to envision himself in the glass bubble of the cockpit, waving down at crowds of enthusiastic supporters. No, Thomas would not dare fly in such an ominous machine, but he felt a surge of exhilaration at the thought.

He stopped for a moment, and Mary Lee gave him a quizzical stare, which he ignored. He wanted to preserve this moment. His lovely wife before him, a son with so much potential next to her. Even if Tommy was wearing the wrong socks.

And up there, inside the Red Room the daring congressman–perhaps a future senator–waited inside. A man who, with some good fortune, might soon be one of the three most powerful men in Texas. At that moment Thomas felt part of a larger world, with Cottonwood no longer an insignificant town in East Texas, but as important, for tonight, as any place in New York or Washington.

His wife was no less lovely than the women who might be gathered at political functions there, and his feelings, expansive as they were, would rival those of any man.

He smiled at Mary Lee. "Ready?" he said. She took his arm and smiled back. Surprise crossed her face, and in that moment she seemed to blossom. Confidently, Thomas escorted her towards the stairs. Tommy followed behind.

The Red Room held two different crowds of Cottonwood's finest. They divided naturally, one group to the left, gathered around a punch bowl in the center of a white cloth-covered table. There, a Negro man in a cream-colored jacket ladled some green, foamy concoction from the punch bowl into clear glass cups.

Thomas spotted the school superintendent and his wife next to the town's two rival Baptist preachers. He nodded at his dentist, a big-wig in the local Rotary Club, who was head to head with the president of the new junior college. A couple of doctors and their wives huddled off to one side, their backs turned to an overbearing banker that most everyone tried to avoid.

A similar set up dominated the opposite end of the Red Room–the same white cloth-covered table and an almost identical Negro man serving drinks. But he poured the drinks for those gathered there from quart bottles of Jack Daniels and Wild Turkey and jugs of rosé wine. Out to one side cans of Jax and Falstaff beer floated in a tub among chunks of ice.

This group was louder and more careless in their gestures. Thomas nodded when Vernon Paroline raised a glass his way. Robert Newsome, a bandage across his forehead, was nose to nose with a sharply dressed, full-figured woman that Thomas didn't recognize, an aide to Congressman Johnson, he suspected. Newsome glanced quickly at Thomas, but did not acknowledge his presence.

A couple of teenage boys inspected the stage–really no more than a low platform covered with a scrap of a rug–that took up one corner of the room. One of them tapped the microphone lightly while the other one knelt down to check out the amplifier.

So there would be a barbecue brisket dinner, with the predictable cole slaw and potato salad and beans, and later the band would take over, and the Red Room would become a dance hall, of sorts. None of that interested Thomas in the least, although at the proper time he would not turn down a slice of lean brisket.

Thomas studied the crowded room once more. Lyndon Johnson was nowhere to be seen. Thomas vacillated a minute between the two groups. He certainly wouldn't hang around the drinkers; alcohol–with its attendant loss of control–had never appealed to him at all.

But the crowd at the other end of the room, sipping their punch with foam from melted lime sherbet floating on top like so much scum, appealed even less. Thomas considered their piety an abomination. And boring, too. The mood around the punch bowl felt brittle enough to shatter.

He would wait. He would wait here in the center of the room and drink nothing, not throwing his allegiance to either group. When the barbecue was served he would have a glass of sweet iced tea.

At one end of the veranda a black portable pit churned out smoke. From the Red Room and through the open doors Thomas could make out ghost-like men moving around the pit, with Tommy, always eager for a meal, right in the middle. The boy would never get rid of the smoke. It would cling forever to his clothes and hair. Oh, well, Thomas thought. It's too late. He sighed. And, yes. I'm too hard on the boy; I need to let up on him. With that silent admission he shook his head and looked away.

Down at the other end of the veranda four men dressed in fringed western costumes stood in a circle, oversized hats almost touching, tuning fiddles and guitars. The first few notes of the Orange Blossom Special reverberated from the veranda into the Red Room, and then suddenly died out.

In between the barbecue pit and the band several dozen tables were set up, covered with white butcher paper. Jars of peppers and pickles and a bowl of barbecue sauce took up the center of each table, along with a small loaf of Mrs. Baird's sliced white bread.

There was nowhere that Thomas felt comfortable, and he glanced back at the entrance. Maybe he would step outside again. But Mary Lee was still by his side, and she wouldn't understand at all. No, he resolved. He would stay put. Here.

A hand slapped his back and Thomas turned to face a grinning Vernon Paroline. "Well, if it isn't the counselor," Vernon said. He extended his hand to Thomas and simultaneously leaned towards Mary Lee for a kiss he didn't get. "My, my," he said, pulling back. He swirled the ice cubes in his glass. "And a lucky counselor at that." He laughed. "Well, lucky may not tell the entire story."

"Luck is what fools rely on," Thomas said. "It has nothing to do with my life."

Mary Lee squeezed Thomas's arm. "There's Kate," she said, her eyes widening in disbelief at Vernon's lack of tact. "I'll be right back."

"The congressman," Vernon said, pausing a minute while he watched Mary Lee hurry away. The heels of her satin pumps clicked on the wooden floor. The peplum that flared over her hips swayed as she moved across the room. "I hear," Vernon finally continued, "that he's sulking. Pouting. Yeah, things didn't go just how the big man wanted and so he's holed up in his room upstairs. Word is he's already in his pj's. And in his cups, too. Sipping Johnnie Walker Black. That's what that Chudars fellow says."

Vernon leaned close. Thomas smelled stale cigarette smoke, a blending of sweet bourbon and Coke. "Chudars is Johnson's helicopter pilot. The fellow over there, in that flowerdy sport shirt. He's visiting with Coach Joe Mack again, bending his ear for sure. Bet I end up with a bunch more stories."

Thomas glanced Chudars' way. The pilot was a non-descript looking fellow, lean and tan and probably a veteran. Thomas could easily see him in an Army Air Corps uniform. Chudars seemed to be a little bored with Coach Green and the whole affair.

"He's pissed as all get out with the big man," Vernon said. He fingered a new pack of Camels, slipping it over and over in his palm before tucking the pack into his jacket pocket. "Johnson, I hear, threatened to let him go if he didn't land that chopper downtown, where all the folks were.

"Chudars told him hell no. 'I'm no damned fool,' is what Chudars said. His actual words, as Joe Mack tells it. The fly-boy warned the congressman that there was light wires strung all over the place, down there. Hell, any fool could see that.

"And you know what Johnson said?" Vernon asked. He reached out and grabbed the sleeve of Thomas's coat, pulling him close. "Told him electric wires was his friends. Said that his platform was practically built on rural electrification. Can you believe that? That Johnson. He's a cockeyed cutter. A case and a half, if you ask me."

"I need to check with Robert," Thomas said, nodding towards the county attorney. He tried to pull away from Vernon.

"Hey, don't go yet," Vernon said. "Did Mary Lee tell you that I gave that old worn out Ford of yours the once over this afternoon? A pretty gal like that, she sure deserves a new Ford. And I can make you a deal."

Thomas wanted to ask Vernon where in the world he had seen Mary Lee and the Ford, but he didn't care enough to put up with the man's mindless ramblings. Finally he worked free of Vernon's grasp and moved towards the crowd huddled around the liquor table.

When the three of them had stopped in the center of the Red Room, Tommy checked the crowd, hoping that Gene was there. He was afraid to even hope that he might spot Zoette, watching for him to show up. But the room was half-filled with mostly old people. A couple of guys he knew from school were messing with the microphone, but they were older and played in the marching band.

Tommy slipped away from his parents and headed for the veranda. He moved through the tall doorway and to the far end, wanting to get another look at the helicopter before dark. It was a hundred feet or so away, parked in an open area next to the ninth green. If Gene showed up they would slip down there and give it a close-up inspection.

He shed his suit coat and folded it over the stone wall at the veranda's edge. He loosened his tie and wandered back around the tables to the barbecue pit. "Man," he said to a fellow who had his head stuck halfway in the pit. "That sure does smell good."

"Hey, Tommy," he said. It was Oran Holley. "You need a sample?"

"Gene told me you might be here," Tommy said. "And yeah, I sure could use something. Man, I'm starving."

Oran laughed. "You're just like Gene. He told me to tell you he couldn't make it. Not tonight. He's helping out at the stand downtown. My old lady's running it for now. But she'll be along later. She said she wouldn't miss a party–not out here. Yeah, Gene can take care of things the last couple of hours when things slow down."

Oran stepped back from the pit. "We're not the country club sort, you know. Not our kind of crowd." He looked serious for a minute, then lightened up again.

"Truth is, I suspect my old lady wants to keep her eye on me." He gave Tommy a wink. "All these pretty women. I hear there's some wild parties."

Oran forked a slab of brisket and plopped it on a cutting board. "Now I'll show you something," he said. He sliced the end off the brisket and held it up with his two-pronged fork. "The thickness of this smoke ring–see here, at the edge of the meat." He pointed to the strip of pink-tinged meat just under the crusty edge of the brisket. "This tells you how long the brisket has smoked. The wider the ring, the longer it smoked. This one looks like a rainbow."

He nodded and slid the strip of brisket onto a paper plate. "Try this," he said. "I use green oak down there in the firebox, and the smoke rises up through the flue to the smoke chamber." He closed the heavy lid. "Made this contraption myself."

"Man, this is great." Tommy licked the drippings off his fingers. "Thanks a lot, Mr. Holley. I sure was hoping Gene could make it." He shrugged. "When will we get to eat?"

"When the big man comes down those stairs," Oran said, pointing his fork to the wide rock steps that led to the guest apartments above. That's what they tell me, anyway. Sure hope he gets himself in gear. I can't keep this brisket moist forever."

"Well," Tommy said, "while I'm waiting, I think I'll go check out that helicopter."

"Don't be flying off in that eggbeater," Oran said. He glanced at the sky. "It's already too dark to fly. You hear?"

Tommy grinned. "No way," he said, and he took off, trotting towards the winding back stairs.

Up close the helicopter looked too bulky to get off the ground. Tommy walked around it a couple of times, running his hand across the smooth finish. He reached up to touch the drooping blades and envisioned them starting their whomp, whomp, whomp, lifting the helicopter slowly into the air. He glanced around, then tried the door to the cockpit. It wasn't locked, and he pulled it half open. He could sit there in the pilot's seat if he wanted to. But he was afraid of getting caught and he pushed the door shut until it clicked.

He wandered out on the smoothness of the ninth green. From there he could take in most of the veranda, the smoke still rising in white puffs whenever Oran Holley lifted the barbecue pit's sheet metal lid. As he watched, a procession of Negro men appeared up there, toting oblong serving dishes heavy with beans and cole slaw and potato salad. They lined them up on the serving table next to a couple of insulated iced tea dispensers.

Tommy was starved but wasn't in a hurry to leave the squishy grass of the green. He moved to the hole in the center of the green and held the pin, pretending that some famous golfer, maybe Ben Hogan, was putting to win the PGA championship and Tommy was his caddy. He slipped the pin from the hole as the imaginary ball rolled his way and plopped into the cup.

Tommy glanced around, hoping that no one had seen this charade, but it was good dark now, and he was alone. In one of the third floor apartments a light came on, and someone parted the drapes. It was a man, and as he leaned towards the window he enclosed his face with his hands, peering out into the night. "Lyndon Johnson," Tommy whispered. He recognized him from the afternoon's fiasco at the junior college grounds.

The congressman suddenly whipped around and pointed his finger, jabbing it in the air at someone across the room and out of Tommy's sight. When Johnson turned back the bathrobe he wore billowed open at his chest.

Tommy lifted the flag and waved it at the window. He devised a code of his own, moving the flag in semaphore style, up and down, waving it from side to side in tricky ways. "This message is for Congressman Johnson," he whispered as the flag cut through the air. "Get dressed. Immediately. Go downstairs so that the dinner can begin."

He stopped then, his arms aching from the effort to communicate with Lyndon Johnson, and stuck the pin back in the hole. When he looked up the congressman had disappeared. Tommy watched the window for a while. Every now and then a shadow moved across a far wall.

Then all at once Johnson appeared back at the window. Now he was dressed and was using the window as a mirror while he tightened his tie. Someone came up behind him, holding his suit coat open and Johnson slipped his arms back into the sleeves and shrugged the coat into place. He moved away, once more jabbing the air with his finger, and then the light in the apartment clicked off.

Tommy stroked an imaginary putt towards the pin, and when it fell, dead center in the hole, he trotted towards the club house and his barbecue dinner.

When Mary Lee spotted Kate across the Red Room, she hurried towards her, relieved to leave Thomas to deal as best he could with Vernon Paroline. But she couldn't say anything about Vernon to Kate, not yet, since her friend was stuck between Rita Paroline and Coach Green's wife, Darlene.

Mary Lee joined them, going through the routine of the insincere, but expected acknowledgments of each other's presence. "How are you?" and "So good to see you." Nods and smiles and quick appraisals ricocheted through the circle of women.

Darlene Green was an attractive woman with striking red hair that fell past her shoulders. But she had the annoying habit of running her fingers through her hair and tossing it back from her face while she talked. The constant movement drove Mary Lee crazy.

"Oh, Darlene," Kate said. "I would give a fortune to have hair like that." She laughed. "If I had one, that is."

Rita leaned close to Mary Lee. "You poor dear," she said.

"How are you holding up? With all the strain of this horrible business with that nigra boy."

Before Mary Lee could answer, Kate turned to Rita. "What a lovely dress," she said. "Where in the world did you find it?"

Rita beamed. "Do you think so? I picked it up at the last minute. We were in Tyler, on business." She held her hand up to her face as if to whisper some major secret. "Vernon just may be branching out, the Ford dealership over there is available. But don't tell a soul. Vernon would kill me. Anyway, I didn't know if I would have time to stop by your shop when we got back. Vernon was taking so long. He goes on and on, you know. So, well, there's that little shop over there, out on Broadway. The White Magnolia. And . . . oh, do you really like it?"

Kate smiled. Her "I could kill you" smile.

The dress is dreadful, Mary Lee thought, and you're a witch besides. "Kate," she said. "Can you help me with something?" Mary Lee reached behind her back and touched the zipper. "In the powder room. It won't take a minute." She turned to Rita and Darlene. "Be right back."

"Oh, don't hurry," Rita said with her too nice to be believed smile. "We need to refresh our drinks, anyway."

Alone in the powder room Kate exploded. "The nerve of that woman. First she insults you. Then flaunts that tacky dress in front of me. The White Magnolia, my eye. She sewed that herself from a McCalls' pattern. In 1940 at that."

Mary Lee tried to control herself, then laughed nervously. She resolved to ignore Rita's catty remarks about Thomas' problems. If she blew up and told Rita off it would ruin everything.

"Oh," Mary Lee said. "You don't care for hibiscus patterns? The blossoms are so huge. And pink and white are your favorite colors, I thought."

"Walking wallpaper," Kate said. "That's what she looks like."

"Nasty, nasty," Mary Lee said, wagging her finger at her friend.

"Absolutely and unrepentantly nasty. Guilty as charged."

Mary Lee checked the seam of her nylons in the full length mirror. She touched her nose and cheeks with the lightest puff of powder from her compact.

"Perfect," Kate said. "Now first I need a big glass of that rosé wine, and then on to the dinner. This is your big night, you know."

"Oh, God. Yes, it is. I suppose."

"Thomas has no expectations," Kate told her, "except that you look lovely and act graciously. The lovely part is no problem. Just look at yourself. And if I can keep you and Rita separated, the gracious part will be easy."

"You're such a friend," Mary Lee said as they pushed back into the clamor of the Red Room.

"A friend, yes. But, insatiably curious, too." Kate laughed. "I'll be watching your every move."

A glass of wine might help, Mary Lee thought. She dug around in her purse for the tiny bottle of April in Paris perfume she saved for special occasions. A dab more behind each ear should camouflage her wine breath. She would drink just one glass with Kate and not tell Thomas, who wouldn't approve.

And from out of nowhere she remembered sipping a warm beer that night, all of those years ago, in Horace Ledbetter's Pontiac coupe out at Tyler State Park. The slight dizziness she felt then had alarmed her at first, the string of lights above the dance floor appearing to move, to wave against the night sky even when Mary Lee sat as still as possible.

But the dizziness had not been unpleasant, and for some time afterwards she had longed to recapture that momentary feeling of euphoria. She felt daring at the time and had experienced longings that she would never, ever tell anyone about.

Certainly not Thomas, and not even Kate. Well, maybe given the right circumstance she might confide her secret thoughts to Kate.

Thomas was still nodding while Vernon Paroline jabbered on, and Mary Lee followed Kate to the liquor table and discreetly helped herself to a stemmed glass of pink wine. Kate moved towards the veranda, and Mary Lee followed, carefully positioning the wine glass out of her husband's sight.

For a few minutes the two women stood at the open door, sipping their wine, their backs to the chatter of the Red Room. Lightning far to the southeast lit up the horizon, then disappeared. The wine was cool and sweet, then smooth and warm. Mary Lee felt that long ago lightness and rested her free hand on the frame of the door.

"Zip-A-Dee-Doo-Dah," Kate said. "This is better." She held her half-empty glass up.

"My, oh my, yes," Mary Lee laughed. "Zip-A-Dee-Doo-Dah without a doubt. 'Everything is satisfactual.'"

"Bottoms up," Kate said, lifting her glass in a toast. "I'll get us a couple more."

"Kate," Mary Lee said. She felt leggy–not taller–for the floor seemed to be no farther away. But her legs wanted to move, to flash. "I have to be proper. Thomas would have a conniption fit."

"He'll never know," Kate said. "No one will. I'll sneak the next ones." Kate slipped back towards the bar, where she sidled up to the table and discreetly lifted two full glasses of wine. A shoplifter in the Smart Shoppe could not have been smoother.

Mary Lee giggled as she watched her friend. She moved farther out on the veranda and eased her empty glass onto one of the tables.

"Mary Lee Patterson," a man behind her said, and she whirled around. She had been caught–by Byron Bostick.

He glanced at the glass on the table behind Mary Lee. "I've been wanting to talk to you," he said.

"Oh, yes," Mary Lee said. "I should have called. I know I said I would. But it's been so crazy at our house, and I'm really not sure what to do. I have been studying the real estate manual, though. And I keep telling Thomas that I might want to try . . ."

Byron held up his hand. "Don't worry, Mary Lee. It's okay," he said. Byron was so earnest, so sincere. His brown eyes drew Mary Lee in. He seemed to be a man that Mary Lee could trust, one that she could even like. As a friend. She could work for this man.

"Real estate is a tricky business," he said. "You're up one day and down the next. Especially in small towns. I mean there's just so much money here, and only so many houses. The old land you can hardly give away."

"Oh," Mary Lee said. "I would have a lot to learn. But Thomas could help me with all the legal part, and I could brush up on my math, and we were talking, just today, about getting a better car–better for taking clients around, you know."

"Well," Byron said. "That's all fine. And, who knows? Things might work out. But later. Not right now with things so slow. It wouldn't be fair to you."

"Oh," Mary Lee said. "I see. I guess." I am getting the brush-off, she thought. This is not about real estate in Cottonwood, it's about Thomas and Chester and Corrine. And how Mary Lee, who is connected to all of that sordid mess, might hurt his business. He can't fool me.

"I knew you would understand," Byron said.

Just then Kate returned with the drinks, and Mary Lee stepped towards her and defiantly took her glass. "Well," she said. "Here's to, here's to . . ." but she could not come up with the right toast. She wanted something to take Byron Bostick down a notch or two. The perfect words would come to her, she knew, later, probably at three in the morning.

Byron nodded at Kate. He gave Mary Lee a quick wink, and in a moment disappeared back inside the Red Room.

"What was that all about?" Kate asked. "That wink? I don't trust that man."

"Oh, Kate. I think this whole thing is worse than I thought. Maybe I'd better get Thomas and Tommy. We don't belong here, and everyone–except you–seems to be against us. I feel like giving up."

"Give it a chance, hon," Kate said. "Let's step over to the wall and count the stars. We'll finish off wine number two and things will look a whole lot better. Remember, Madame Acton is on your side."

"Well," Mary Lee said as they moved across the veranda. "If things don't start looking up, I'll try to get my five dollars back."

⁂

Thomas moved away from Vernon, working through the room towards Robert Newsome. He waited while the four Bunkhouse Boys, carrying their instruments above their western hats, pushed their way past him on their way towards the stage. A sprinkling of applause rippled through the hard liquor end of the Red Room.

Robert Newsome had his back turned to the veranda, and the big-boned woman across from him kept glancing over his shoulder towards the open doors, absently nodding as he droned on and on.

Just as Thomas reached them the woman sighed, "Thank God," and Lyndon Johnson strode into the room, the crowd parting as if by magic. The woman hurried away, leading Lyndon to the stage where she elbowed the lead Bunkhouse Boy away from the microphone. "The next United States senator from the great state of Texas, folks. Lyndon Baines Johnson." She gave a surprising whoop and handed Johnson a note card, then led the room in energetic applause.

The Bunkhouse Boys caught the spirit of the moment and managed the first few bars of "The Eyes of Texas" before the congressman took the stage.

From what Vernon Paroline had told him, Thomas assumed that Johnson would be in a foul mood and half tipsy, but there he stood, fresh as a May morning, his smile wide and sincere. He stretched his arms out, as if he wanted to gather in everyone assembled there.

The congressman was a big man, taller than Thomas had realized, and the platform stage where he stood accentuated his height. He wore a gray sharkskin suit and shiny-toed western boots. His tie, with its colorful but unidentifiable design, stood out against his starched white shirt. His slick-backed hair, with little waves curling above his over-sized ears, gleamed under the glow from the chandeliers.

Thomas expected a speech, but Johnson was too smart for that. The congressman must have realized that his earlier contrariness had held the party up–he would have noticed the barbecue buffet ready to go when he moved across the veranda. So he thanked the crowd for coming, a genuine appreciation, it seemed, the big man moving his head from side to side as he talked in an attempt to make eye contact with everyone there.

Johnson slipped his glasses on and paused long enough to check the note card that his aide had earlier handed him. He thanked by name the board of directors of the country club, asking them to raise their hands, and they did. Vernon Paroline raised his empty glass.

Johnson searched the crowd a moment, and Thomas tightened a little, hoping that he might be included in the candidate's list of notable locals. "And a Texas-sized thanks to Robert Newsome, the county Democratic chairman."

Newsome waved his arm weakly and nodded, before killing off the last of his bourbon. Johnson paused a moment then, a dramatic pause that utilized his perfect sense of timing. "I'm not one to dilly-dally around," he said, "when there's a plate of barbecue waiting for me." He chuckled at his own humor. "So I propose that you folks refresh your drinks and we head out to the veranda. And, who knows, after supper, I might even try to talk one of these charming Cottonwood women into a waltz, if the Bunkhouse Boys will oblige us."

Those gathered around the punch bowl shook their heads in disapproval, but the hard liquor end of the room yelped and applauded.

"There'll be time enough for politics after we take care of what's important," he said, and with the wave of his hand, stepped down next to his aide.

The crowd whooped their appreciation and headed for the veranda doors. The band broke into a fast-paced rendition of "The Orange Blossom Special" that had half the crowd dancing out into the night.

This is my moment, Thomas thought, for he could see that Johnson and his aide were now head to head in an animated exchange, seemingly not concerned about getting to the barbecue spread at all. Thomas side-stepped his way against the surge of the crowd, wanting to get to the congressman before Robert Newsome could claim his attention.

As he moved towards Johnson he glanced around for Mary Lee. This would be a fine opportunity for her to meet the candidate, but no, she had disappeared, probably caught up in some frivolous jabber with Kate.

When Thomas approached the pair, Johnson looked up. His reading glasses were still perched on his nose, and Thomas caught a glimpse of a paper he had been going over. BRIEFING was at the top of the page and LONGVIEW, TEXAS just below.

It obviously was tomorrow's agenda. He's going through the motions here, Thomas realized. Another perfunctory whistle stop on that long campaign run.

But just like that, Johnson turned his attention to Thomas, as if Cottonwood had been his ultimate destination and Thomas the most important player in this election game.

Johnson reached out and grasped Thomas's hand, completely enveloping it in his own huge grip, and Thomas suddenly felt small and weak, but managed to introduce himself. "I'm running in the Democratic primary," he added. "The race for state district judge."

Johnson nodded and his eyes lit up, whether in genuine or fake recognition, Thomas could not tell.

"I am campaigning, too," Thomas said. "Although on a very small scale. And, if you recall, you wrote me a letter of commendation last year, for the way I handled a criminal case here in Cottonwood."

Johnson nodded again. "Yes, yes," he said. "I do remember that." He shot his aide an impatient look. "Dorothy," he said. "A copy of that letter."

Dorothy frantically leafed through a spiral notebook. Her lips moved as she murmured 'Patterson, Patterson, Patterson' and her finger raced down each page.

"I certainly will appreciate your support," Johnson said. The congressman stepped closer and with his left hand grasped the lapel of Thomas's coat. He jabbed a finger into his chest. "We have to work together," Johnson said. "Get the voters out, lined up to support us. Old Coke Stevenson and his cronies will scare the daylights out of folks if we don't set the record straight." Johnson lessened his grip, but didn't let go, and didn't step back an inch. Thomas could smell whiskey and peppermint mouth wash.

"Now let me give you some advice. You don't have to be the handsomest man in the race, or even the smartest, but if you plan to win you goddamned sure have to be the hardest working."

Dorothy looked up from her notebook. She had wide set eyes and thin brown bangs that looped down over her high forehead. She wore a "Don't mess with me, Buster" look on her face. Thomas could see that she was used to protecting, defending, and advising her boss. She sized Thomas up, a frown on her face. She held out the notebook for Johnson to see.

The congressman released his grip on Thomas's coat and stepped back. He took a minute to read over Dorothy's shoulder. "Oh, I see, I see," he said. "Now I remember. Yes, I did write a letter of commendation." He glanced over at Thomas and pulled his glasses down. "But I hear that circumstances have changed." He pulled on one of his drooping earlobes.

"Congressman Johnson," Thomas said, "Circumstances have changed. But through no fault of my own. I am still the man you praised last year, and with your endorsement, I believe I can put this behind me and become a sterling–if I may be so immodest–state district judge. One that the Democratic party can be proud of. A progressive in the mold of FDR and Harry Truman, and of you, sir."

"An endorsement," Johnson said, working the word around in his mouth as if he could taste it. "Those are not to be given lightly. I may need to investigate the ramifications. Oh, politics can be awful tedious sometimes."

He glanced at Dorothy, who frowned and gave a barely imperceptible sideways shake of her head. "This is not an easy one," he finally said. "In fact, it's goddamned hard."

But then he got a big grin on his face, as if he and Thomas were the best of pals who had not one problem in the world. "You know, I need a plate of that barbecue, and Robert Newsome over there has promised that I would get my fill. I can't disappoint the county Democratic chairman, now can I? We'll have to finish this later," he said. "Nothing is impossible on a full stomach. You can understand that, I'm sure."

"Dorothy," he said to his aide. "Two fingers. Johnnie Walker Black." He gestured towards the bar with two meaty fingers. She closed the notebook with a finality that jarred Thomas and hurried off to fetch her boss a drink.

Johnson clapped Thomas on the shoulder, holding his hand there for a moment as if to keep him situated in place, stuck at that spot. Then the big man strode across the room and disappeared onto the veranda, Dorothy chasing after him with his drink.

The Bunkhouse Boys started up "Arkansas Traveler," and Thomas retreated towards the empty front porch. He wanted to leave, to go . . . but where? Not home. He couldn't bear to drag Mary Lee home where he would have to explain how all was lost, how his best and last effort had absolutely failed.

And he was sick of his office and his lists and his failed strategies. There was nowhere for Thomas to go, so he moved out the front door and sank down on the steps. From there the clink and clatter, the talk and music mingled hazily behind him, rising and falling, as if the sounds rode lightly on some strange and sour wind.

Tommy stayed out on the veranda while Johnson stepped up on the stage to give his talk–he was determined to be first in line for the barbecue. But he knew how politicians could go on and on and was afraid that Johnson might make up for the afternoon's abbreviated speech with a long-winded one tonight.

So he wandered to the far end of the veranda and eased himself up on the rock wall. From there, the second floor of the clubhouse, he could sit and watch the helicopter on the ground below. A single pale light bulb was strung across the dark, casting a light that played across the grass towards the helicopter.

The wind whiffled across the veranda, the edges of tablecloths flapping like wings of white birds. By the light of the half moon Tommy watched as the helicopter gently rocked, its blades coming alive in the spring wind.

"The Orange Blossom Special" woke Tommy from his reverie, and, when he swung his legs back around, the crowd burst onto the veranda, dancing and jostling for positions next to the buffet. By the time Tommy could get there twenty or so people had secured their places in front of him.

Oran Holley served the brisket, sliding slices onto each plate and smothering them with a ladle of chocolate-colored sauce. When Tommy finally shuffled by, Oran slipped an extra slice of beef on Tommy's plate and gave him a wink. By the time he made it through the line, Tommy's plate was overflowing with brisket and all the trimmings.

He looked around for a place to sit, but his father was not around, and his mother and Kate were still far back in the line talking and nodding. His mother held a wine glass. He had never seen her drink wine, and for some reason he didn't want to, and turned away.

There were a couple of places at a long table, but there was no way he would share a table with any old strangers. Another table was filling up with a group of school teachers that had beat him to the line. He'd rather not eat at all than sit with them. He was on his own, he guessed.

So he picked up a glass of sweet iced tea and moved back to his place on the rock wall. He swung around, his feet dangling over the edge, a dozen feet above the ground. He tucked a napkin into his collar and tore a piece of brisket apart with his fork. Man, he thought, this is some spread. I hope they give you seconds.

He checked the helicopter again and there, shadowed in the half moon light with one hand on her hip, stood Zoette, impatiently waving at him. She wore a dress, kind of a party dress, Tommy guessed, for it was red and shone like satin. When she hurried over to the wall he could hear it rustle.

"I thought you'd never see me," she said. "I've been waving and waving, but all you could do was keep your eyes on that plate."

Tommy checked behind to make sure he was alone. "Well come on up here. The barbecue's great. What are you doing out there, anyway?"

"You come down here," she said. "There's a bench over there, by that green. I'd feel funny up there."

Tommy didn't get that, but he nodded. "Be right there," he said.

By the time he made it down the stairs Zoette had settled onto the bench. She kicked her shoes off and re-tied a red ribbon that held back her hair.

Tommy eased down next to her. He held the plate out. "Help yourself," he said. "We can share."

"Oh, I'm not hungry," Zoette said. But in a minute she pinched off a piece of brisket. "Not bad," she said. "We don't eat barbecue much."

"Gosh," Tommy said. "I thought you weren't going to make it." The neckline of her dress was all red ruffles that dipped low, teasing Tommy's eyes. Once he thought he glimpsed the swell of her breast, but in the dim light he couldn't be sure. He tried to keep his eyes on Zoette's eyes–he strained to make contact when she looked at him–but as soon as she looked away his eyes fell to her neckline again. He couldn't help himself.

"Why did you stay down here instead of coming on up for the reception, the barbecue and everything? You're all dressed up for a party."

"I was going to. I went to the front door and peeked in, but I didn't see you."

"Aw," Tommy said. "I guess I was out here by the helicopter."

"Anyway," Zoette said. "I did see this preacher–the skinny man with the loud voice. He came out to see Mama a few weeks ago–him and some other men. They stood right there at the door and told Mama she was a servant of the devil. I was there, right beside her all the time. That skinny preacher gave her holy-what-for until she finally slammed the door in his face. I didn't want to run into him for sure."

"Aw, him," Tommy said. "My father can't stand him either. Don't worry, though. He'll be taking off as soon as the dancing starts. Maybe we can go up there and watch."

Zoette nodded and seemed to fade away to her own dream world for a minute.

"My buddy Gene told me that you're fifteen," Tommy said. "Is that right?"

"Sixteen in August," Zoette said. "I hate it, being the oldest in my grade. It's all that moving around we do. I've been in twelve schools already, and some of them don't like it when you come in late in the year and have to catch up. I was in the fourth grade for two years. One grade in five different schools."

"Man," Tommy said. "I don't see how you could do that."

"When I'm seventeen I'm quitting, leaving home. It's not any fun, the way people talk about my mama, her fortune telling and all."

"I could leave home, too," Tommy said. "Some days I think I might just drive off in the Ford and not come back. My father wants me to be a lawyer, but I don't know why. Being a lawyer sure doesn't seem to make him happy."

"I'm going to be an actress," Zoette said. She nibbled the edges of a pickle slice, staring at the sky. "I have a cousin who lives in Chicago and she's an actress. Maybe I can live with her for a while."

"Chicago doesn't seem like a good place for an actress," Tommy said. "I think you ought to go to Hollywood."

"Maybe. You can't tell." She turned back to Tommy. He had started to sop the barbecue sauce with a piece of bread, but he waited. "Are your parents happy?" she asked. "Do you think they're really happy?"

Tommy hadn't ever thought about that. They were just his parents. "I guess," he said. But then, as soon as he said it, he knew that wasn't right. "Well, maybe not. I guess they argue a lot. And Mother sometimes yells and stomps around after my father drives off to his office. Maybe my parents are too old to be happy."

Zoette laughed. "Maybe. No, they don't sound very happy to me."

"How about you?" Tommy asked. "Are your folks happy?"

"They don't even pretend," she said. "Not any more. I'm not going to be that way though. I won't ever marry–famous actresses don't have to–and I'll make a lot of money and buy a big house. I'll live there forever. There'll be no cruddy trailer for me."

Tommy licked his fingers and pulled his napkin out of his collar. He wiped his hands and started to fold the napkin, but he wadded it up instead.

"Do you know the stars?" Zoette asked. "I mean all the constellations and all the planets and everything?"

"The big dipper," Tommy said. "And the Milky Way, and maybe Saturn."

"I know all about the stars," Zoette said, "the way they change in the sky, the way they affect what we do and how we act." She jumped up. "Come on," she said. "Let's lie down there, on the green where it's soft. I will show you the stars. If you tell me when you were born, I can tell your fortune in a different way."

Tommy couldn't believe it. Zoette Acton had asked him to lie down with her alone, in the dark. Tommy Patterson, on the ninth green of the Cottonwood Country Club, alone with an almost sixteen-year-old girl who probably would be a famous actress someday. This was much better than going back upstairs for seconds.

A barbecue dinner on the veranda of the country club would normally be a lively affair, with beer bottles stacking up in the big barrel by the stairs, and lies being told by tipsy men who hugged women who were not their wives a little too long.

But when Lyndon Johnson carried a heaping plate of barbecue to the table set for six, everyone who had gathered on the veranda got quiet. They watched and listened while the congressman held forth to those around him–Robert Newsome, of course, and Vernon Paroline and Rita, since Vernon and Lyndon Johnson both had vested interests in more black-top roads throughout the state.

Dorothy, the aide, sat to Lyndon's left, monitoring his intake of Johnnie Walker Black as best she could, while going over the schedule for Sunday, the following day. "Sunday be hanged," Johnson had said when one of his advisors had suggested he not campaign on the Lord's Day so not to offend the Baptists. His drive already was legend, and for the next several weeks every day counted. He would not let something as minor as a Sunday ground him and his whirlybird.

Joe Mack Green and Darlene sat across from Johnson, the coach and his wife last minute fill-ins when Thomas Patterson had fallen from political grace. Dorothy and Robert Newsome had worked up the seating arrangements beforehand, but Johnson had insisted on the coach and his wife joining them.

For when Dorothy had briefed Johnson about his choices, she noted that Governor Jester had put Coach Green in his place earlier in the day. Johnson liked that. He figured Joe Mack would be docile now. And he needed a school teacher at his table to emphasize his education platform, but one who wouldn't bring up questions about new taxes and higher salaries and such.

As a plus, Coach Green wasn't afraid of public opinion–he would down a few beers whenever he wanted to–unlike the other teachers in town who had cowered behind the punch bowl at the teetotaler end of the Red Room.

In the subdued atmosphere of the dinner Mary Lee whispered to Kate. She had saved a chair for Thomas, tilted it forward against the table, but he hadn't shown up to claim it. "I don't know whether to be annoyed or worried," she whispered. "It's not like Thomas to be late–for anything."

"Oh, be annoyed," Kate said, sloshing the wine in her glass. "It's so much more rewarding than worrying. Thomas is all right. He's probably back at his office right now, devising some new strategy."

Mary Lee shrugged. The two glasses of wine made it hard to focus on the plate of barbecue. It was all too much. Too much to eat, even too much to look at. She didn't want to eat, afraid that she would lose her nice buzz if she did.

Suddenly Thomas was next to her, kneeling beside the chair. He looked terrible. "Is anything wrong?" Mary Lee asked. She thought Tommy might have driven off and had a wreck. Or maybe got in trouble fooling around that helicopter. Earlier, when Mary Lee had moved through the buffet line, Oran Holley had winked and said something about Tommy "threatening to fly that eggbeater." She had forgotten all about her son after that. She glanced around the room, and her head spun.

"Have you been drinking?" Thomas asked. He motioned to the glass of wine next to her plate–her third one. It was three-quarters full.

"Sipping," she said. "Trying to be sociable. That's all. It's part of my plan."

"Plans be hanged," Thomas hoarsely whispered. "It's all over. Johnson flat turned his back on me. I'm on the ballot and it's too late to get off. And if I campaign without an endorsement I won't have a chance."

"Oh, God," Kate gasped. She had tried not to listen, but couldn't help herself. She touched Mary Lee's arm.

"Let's leave," Thomas said. "No good can come of this evening. Not now. Maybe in the morning I can come up with something else, some new plan of action." He shook his head and Mary Lee thought he might break down and cry. Thomas had never cried.

"Now Thomas," Mary Lee said. "We can't do that. Just turn tail and sneak out, with everyone watching." She felt the wine buoy her spirits. Suddenly she felt brave. Daring.

"Just get a plate and go through the line," she said. "Calmly. We will eat our dinner and talk to Kate. We will not be humiliated. Not here. Not at this hoe-daddy country club."

❖❖❖

When the Negro help began to carry the empty plates from the tables, the Bunkhouse Boys took the stage in the Red Room once again. They tuned for an interminable time before moving on a "One, two, and a one, two, three" into an upbeat version of "Over the Waves."

That was the signal for the Baptists and the school teachers and the superintendent and his wife, and the rest of the punch bowl crowd to say their goodnights. Johnson stood, and boomed out, "Thank you folks for coming. I sure do appreciate your support."

They hurried out, as if the music and the dancing that would inevitably follow might contaminate them. Johnson sank back in his chair. “Goddamn it now Dorothy. I need one more. Just a light one. A night cap so I can get a few hours of decent sleep.”

When Johnson glanced around the room Dorothy turned away from Johnson and rolled her eyes.

“And another round for my friends here,” he said. “You can stand another one, can’t you, Newsome?” Johnson already knew the easy answer.

Thomas had only nibbled at his dinner. The potato salad was too creamy and the cole slaw too vinegary. The beans could have simmered for another hour. It all ran together on his plate. But he ate, knowing that he might need his strength. His meat loaf sandwich lunch hadn’t been enough–not after the trauma of the dog shit on the car door handle and the dead snake. If he told Mary Lee about those things she would be more sympathetic.

He would tell her later. But for now he needed to be alone. He couldn’t stand Johnson and his booming voice and his outlandish, self-promoting stories. He hoped Coke Stevenson trounced him. “I’ll be right back,” he said.

Mary Lee looked puzzled. “Are you all right?” she asked.

“No,” he said. “I’m not all right. I need to be alone for a while.” He pointed at her almost empty wine glass. “You don’t need to finish that.” Thomas moved through the brightness of the Red Room, his eyes straight ahead, and disappeared out the front door.

“Oh, Mary Lee,” Kate said. “Thomas can be such a crab. I don’t see how you stand it. Oh, that man. He burns me up.”

“Now Kate,” Mary Lee said. “All men burn you up, sooner or later. And this is important. It’s the biggest setback Thomas has ever had.” She patted her lips with her napkin.

They needed a touch up. "Oh, I guess I need to check on him. We really should get Tommy and leave. It won't get any better."

"Oh, let Thomas be," Kate said. "Don't pay him any mind. Let him pout on his own. And finish your wine if you want to. You're not his child, you know." Kate grinned. "Besides, I can get you another one."

Soon the help started folding up tables, popping the legs flat, and sliding them against the wall. They toted the chairs into the Red Room and lined them up around the wall.

"Looks like a junior high dance," Kate said. "This brings back horrible memories. The boys on one side and the girls–except for one or two–left alone on the other side."

"I'll bet you were the one or two," Mary Lee said with a laugh.

"I never was and never will be," Kate said, "those one or two. Twenty years later and the grown-up boys still won't come around."

The two women moved back inside, standing around while the band regrouped and the chairs filled in the perimeter of what would be the dance floor. From there Mary Lee could still hear Lyndon Johnson, boisterous and then intimate, confident and then teasing. He certainly knows how to play a crowd, she thought. Whether to a room or a table.

Johnson called out for another drink. "Just freshen this up, Dorothy. And don't bother with the ice cubes." The whole table laughed as they scraped their chairs back and stood, the last group to leave the veranda.

The lights dimmed and the band started up, a twangy waltz that Mary Lee didn't know. Three or four couples whirled out into the middle of the room. She checked the front entrance, thinking that Thomas might be skulking in the shadows, but he was nowhere to be seen.

In a moment Lyndon burst into the room with Rita, and they spun quickly to the center of the floor, waltzing gracefully. For a big man he was light on his feet, and while he danced he gave Rita all of his attention, whispering to her while they moved, laughing when she laughed.

"He has my vote," Kate said. "I'm for any man who can dance like that. I don't see how he does it wearing those boots. And look at his hands. They're huge," she said. "As big as those hibiscus on Rita's lovely dress."

"Now, Kate," Mary Lee said, but with a laugh.

In mid-dance Lyndon dropped Rita off next to Vernon and grabbed Darlene's hand; she stumbled in her high heels before she caught up with him.

The Bunkhouse Boys started in on "I've Got a Humpty Dumpty Heart," and Byron Bostick came by for Kate. She shrugged and said. "Why not?"

Mary Lee caught her friend's hand as she got up and pulled her close. "I thought you didn't trust that man," she whispered with a smile.

"We're not eloping, hon. And besides, I don't trust any of 'em."

The sky had never been so full of stars and planets and constellations, and the magic of it all left Tommy dizzy. Zoette talked, mostly to herself, while they lay on their backs, stretched out on the close-cut Bermuda grass of the green. She moved beyond what they could see to what wasn't visible, and as she kept on Zoette seemed to be straining for something, some way to get out beyond what she could identify in the dark sky above them. But she finally gave up, it seemed, and took Tommy's hand in hers and they lay there quietly for a long time.

❖❖❖

The scraping of chairs and sliding of tables on the veranda finally got them up. Then the whine of a fiddle began and Zoette locked her arm in Tommy's and whirled him awkwardly around. With a laugh she let go and moved through a quick routine of dips and swirls that left her breathless and laughing.

"Oh, let's go up and watch," she said.

"Those old folks? Dancing? I'd rather stay here, where it's quiet."

"Oh, don't be a party pooper," she said and grabbed his hand again and led him up the hill and past the helicopter to the steps. On the veranda they moved around to one side, where they could watch through a narrow window and not be seen.

It was dark out there, the only light coming from the dimmed chandeliers inside the Red Room. The moon now had moved to the west, hidden behind the top floor of the clubhouse.

Tommy spotted his mother, sitting alone. She was smiling, watching her friend Kate and Byron Bostick trying to keep up with a fast-moving tune. His father wasn't around, which didn't surprise Tommy at all.

"Can you dance?" Zoette asked.

"Not like that," Tommy said. "Not to anything fast." He knew the box step, had practiced it in front of a mirror alone in his bedroom. If they played a box step tune he might try dancing with Zoette, but only out there on the veranda, in the dark.

Lyndon Johnson stood by the bar and twirled a finger in his drink. He was nodding at Robert Newsome, towering over the old fellow. In a minute Johnson licked his finger and jabbed it into Newsome's chest so hard it almost knocked him over.

The band stopped for a minute, the fiddler fanning himself with his hat. The lead guitar player kept motioning towards the doorway where a young fellow stood grinning. "Come on up here," the guitar player said. "Now come on."

He turned to the gathering, the twenty or so who were still there. "Help me get this young'un up on the stage." He clapped and nodded and grinned, and a smattering of applause rose from the dancers.

The young fellow shyly stepped onto the platform. He held a guitar at his side.

"Now let me introduce a neighbor of ours," the Bunkhouse Boy said. "A young fellow from over at Corsicana. He's gonna sit in, try out a tune or two he's been working on." He turned to the young man. "The first time in public for this first song. Am I right?"

The young man nodded and grinned. He couldn't have been more than eighteen, Tommy figured.

"Just wrote this one last month," he said, and moved to the microphone. "My name's Lefty Frizzell, and I sure am glad to be here. Hope you like this song. I call it "Mom and Dad's Waltz."

"What a silly name for a song," Zoette said, but before long, by the time he crooned the opening verse about crying and smiling. Zoette was humming along and Tommy thought she might cry.

Lyndon Johnson moved across the room, headed straight for Mary Lee and Kate. He had shed his suit coat, but his tie was still knotted tight at his neck. "Oh, my God, hon," Kate said. "Looks like it's me or you."

Lyndon didn't hesitate. He spoke right at Kate, but gestured towards Mary Lee. "I've had my eye on your pretty lady friend all night long, and by God I'm going to have this dance."

He didn't ask, just took Mary Lee by the hand and waltzed her onto the floor. A couple of yelps came from the far end of the room, and Mary Lee felt herself blush.

Johnson seemed different up close. His shoulders weren't as wide as she had thought, and he was a little pear-shaped. He smelled of whisky and sweat, but he moved smooth and quick. Mary Lee hadn't danced since . . . when? Maybe that night with Horace Ledbetter. Yes, she remembered the string of lights again, but not through the split windshield of the Pontiac. She had been under them, looking up, the lights swirling above her.

Tommy couldn't believe it. His mother and Lyndon Johnson dancing. His daddy would throw a fit, and Tommy checked around, hoping that Thomas Patterson wouldn't suddenly appear. His mother was laughing now, shaking her head, but in a minute, she moved closer to the congressman so that she could talk right into his big ear.

He got serious for a minute, listening, and he nodded. Then Lyndon whispered something back and shook his head. He grinned then and swung Mary Lee around in a fancy move, admiring her up and down when they pulled apart. But she was back at his ear in a moment, all serious, her head bobbing up and down.

"She's giving him an earful," Tommy said to Zoette. "She better watch what she's doing. My mother gets in trouble sometimes saying too much. That's what Daddy says."

"Looks like she's having fun to me." Zoette said. She held her arms up to Tommy, one on his shoulder and one in his hand.

"I can only box step," he said.

She laughed. "Little kids box step. Here, I'll teach you," and she moved, counting out loud, and he followed her, waltzing across the dark veranda, his eyes on his feet.

When Lefty Frizzell came to the end of the song, he looked around, as if he didn't know what to expect, and for a moment the room was silent. Then somebody yelled out "Man, oh man, that was fine as cherry wine," and the whole room broke out laughing and clapping.

Lefty played three more songs before he bowed out, and through them all Lyndon never took his arm from around Mary

Lee's waist. Between tunes he towered over her, teasing and laughing and praising her fine dancing ability. The man had loads of charm.

By now Mary Lee was exhausted. She had made her pitch for Thomas, going through a whole list of reasons why Lyndon Johnson should endorse her husband. "Endorsements are a serious–and political–matter," he said. "I promise to give it my level-headed consideration. But not now. Not tonight. My head doesn't feel all that level right this minute." He laughed, and they took off once more, the Bunkhouse Boys leading them on a chase around the room to "San Antonio Rose."

One waltz had been enough for Tommy, and for Zoette, too, so they moved back to the door to watch once more. Tommy swore he would practice and get better. If he could learn how to shoot left handed layups driving off of his right foot, he could learn how to waltz.

Thomas had wandered out to his car. The parking lot was still now, after all of the punch bowl crowd had left the club, and he could just pick up the fiddling and laughing from the Red Room behind him. He envied those who could simply let a few drinks melt their problems away. Even Mary Lee seemed to be lighter, less on edge tonight. She may have sipped a little more wine than he thought. Oh, well. He wouldn't begrudge her a little lightness. The day had been rough on both of them.

He slid into the driver's seat of his car. Thomas turned the key and clicked on the radio. He pushed all of the BUICK buttons one by one, but got only garbled static. He spun the tuner, finally picking up a station out of Laredo. An enthusiastic voice was selling baby chicks, a thousand to an order at a bargain price. Thomas shook his head and clicked the radio off. He sat there in silence, watching the half moon fall. He would give

Mary Lee a few minutes more, and then they would leave.

❖❖❖

The Bunkhouse Boys had exhausted themselves and their repertoire and started glancing towards the door. "Just a couple more," the guitar player said, "and we'll be calling it a night."

"Get Lefty back," someone yelled. The Bunkhouse Boys all nodded and grinned, grateful to call in some relief, and in a minute Lefty stepped up again.

Lyndon turned towards the stage. "Play that Mom and Dad song again, will you son?" he said.

"Oh my gosh, Mr. Johnson," Mary Lee said. "I'm pooped. I couldn't dance another waltz if I had to."

"Not Mr. Johnson, honey," he said. "It's Lyndon. Just Lyndon. And, hell, we have to dance. Just one more time. I missed you on this one before."

When Lefty began and Lyndon pulled his mother close, Tommy turned to Zoette. "I can't believe it," he said.

Zoette shrugged. "That's what grown-ups do," she said. "That's the way they are." As if there was nothing she hadn't seen before.

Mary Lee felt as if she were riding a merry-go-round that would never stop. She tried to concentrate on Kate each time she and Lyndon whirled by, hoping to fight off the dizziness she felt.

As the tune wound down Lyndon hummed along, stumbling over the words, as he guided Mary Lee towards the veranda. Just before they whirled out into the darkness Lyndon whispered something that Mary Lee didn't quite catch, but from the look in his eyes she understood what he had said. And at that moment she had a crazy idea–maybe she would fly off with him in that black helicopter, not worrying one bit about risk and loss.

At that moment, when Lyndon whispered to his mother, and they exchanged those looks, gazing into each other's eyes, Tommy saw Mary Lee Patterson as never before. She appeared startled and dazed and daring–or perhaps something else. Tommy couldn't at that moment name what he saw there in his mother's eyes–but whatever it was made him both fearful and ashamed, and he turned his head away.

And in that instant, just as Lyndon waltzed her out onto the veranda, Mary Lee caught a glimpse of Thomas at the front entrance to the Red Room. He didn't appear to be angry, which surprised Mary Lee. Only small and disappointed. And then Thomas turned and was gone. Oh my God, she thought, what have I done?

But she didn't let go of Lyndon, and she didn't look back again. And then she and Lyndon were alone, moving across the stone floor of the veranda, and she floated back to that night with Horace Ledbetter, and she could have been with him again, for there was something about that night she had refused to remember, something she had hidden even from herself for all of those years.

She was angry for forgetting, and blamed herself, and blamed Thomas, but let all of that anger go when Lyndon tightened his arm around her waist. Then they were on the stairs, rising, and Mary Lee seemed to float, not touching the steps at all.

Tommy drove Zoette home. When they passed the Dairy King he started to circle the Ford around under the lights to show Zoette off to the guys who always hung out around there. But he had lost his heart for all of this, somehow, and drove her on home.

The trailer looked crappy to him at night. It was old and worn out and trashy, and he wondered how Zoette could stand to live there.

Later, he thought he remembered her kissing his cheek as she slid away from him, but that didn't seem to matter. At home he parked the Ford out front. The Buick wasn't in the garage.

Tommy slept late the next morning. His father was in the living room, reading the Sunday *Tyler Telegraph.* He didn't look up. Tommy slipped out the comic section, and started to ask where his mother was, but thought he'd better wait.

"Your mother is in Tyler," Thomas said, his eyes not leaving the newspaper. "At Grandma Sutton's for a few days. Your grandmother needed help of some sort–sewing curtains, I think."

Tommy ate a bowl of Rice Krispies at the kitchen table, not reading the comics at all. He concentrated, instead, on the swirl of patterns on the blue linoleum, trying to create images the way he did with clouds, hoping that he could make sense of things. ❖

Chapter Fourteen

It was a couple of weeks before Mary Lee came back. She did telephone Tommy most days, calling late in the morning, long after Thomas had gone off to his office. At first she avoided a truthful explanation, falling back instead on the help she was giving her mother as an excuse to be away.

But, finally she admitted that "a vacation from your father might do us both a world of good." She got quiet. "You understand, Tommy. Don't you? You're old enough to understand."

"I guess so," Tommy said. He could make it okay without his mother, but he sure did miss the Ford.

Thomas drove back and forth to Dallas for several days and shortly announced that he would hire on as one of the in-house attorneys for Republic Bank, writing title opinions and drawing up trusts. A solid and respectable position. The best retirement plan in Texas, everyone said.

Before the primary election in July they moved, Thomas leading the way out of Cottonwood in the Buick and Mary Lee and Tommy following in the Ford. They stopped for gas and hamburgers at the Hi Ho Cafe in Kaufman, and in an hour or so pulled up to a newly constructed house in north Dallas, just off of Mockingbird Lane.

Thomas Patterson found the routine at the bank to his liking. Criminal law had been a mistake–now he could see that. Temperamentally he needed to avoid the messiness and disorder involved in those emotional conflicts. He should never have left Dallas in the first place–his mother, Adelle, always reminded him of that when he dropped by to see her on Sundays.

One Wednesday in July, at his desk in downtown Dallas, Thomas checked the primary election results of the day before in the *Dallas Morning News*. He had finished last in the field of four candidates. This was no surprise, for he had informally withdrawn from the race, even though his name remained on the ballot. But 256 voters had voted for him and he felt some measure of pride that 256 residents in that district still believed that he was an honorable man.

Mary Lee passed her real estate exam and joined a Dallas firm that specialized in new developments. For the next several years she spent most hours of her days at work, discussing carpets and ceramic tile and mortgages. Even her moderate success brought some degree of independence, financial and otherwise. Thomas accepted this without comment and without complaint.

Mary Lee met Kate when she came to Dallas for the Trade Apparel shows, and they had drinks and dinner downstairs at the Adolphus Hotel. Kate had finally remarried, but not the ladies' accessories salesman. She decided that she could trust Byron Bostick after all and, after a honeymoon in Galveston, she settled back into Cottonwood as a respectable woman.

Mary Lee and Kate avoided talking about that night when Lyndon Johnson came to Cottonwood, but afterwards, driving home alone, Mary Lee would hum "Mom and Dad's Waltz" and cry.

Before they left Cottonwood Tommy had driven the Ford out the highway to see Zoette, to tell her good-bye and that he wouldn't be there at Cottonwood High School in the fall. But the trailer was gone, and the old candy factory had a red and white For Sale sign out front. For a while Tommy walked around out back where the trailer had been, hoping he would find something he could keep, an earring or a ribbon, something to remember Zoette by.

Finally he picked up a weathered clothespin and inspected it. This might have held Zoette's scooped-neck blouse, he thought. But it might have held old man Acton's underdrawers as well, he knew, and tossed it towards the blackened trash barrel.

For some years afterwards, even when he went to the movies with the woman who would become his wife, Tommy scanned the credits as they slowly slid down the screen, really believing–at first–that he might spot Zoette's name listed among those who played small parts.

They had all played small parts, he finally decided.

Except for Lyndon Johnson. Did he remember Mary Lee Patterson, Tommy wondered, even these many years later? Every time President Johnson lifted off from the White House lawn in that helicopter, did he remember leaving Mary Lee Patterson behind? Did he remember waltzing that Saturday night with Tommy's mother, a pretty, but slightly confused woman who meant no harm? Would he finally know that despite our best intentions we all do harm? ❖